MELONHEAD

AND THE
LATER GATOR PLAN

MELONHEAD

AND THE
LATER GATOR PLAN

BY KATY KELLY
ILLUSTRATED BY GILLIAN JOHNSON

A YEARLING BOOK

Text copyright © 2015 by Katy Kelly
Cover and interior illustrations copyright © 2015 by Gillian Johnson

All rights reserved. Published in the United States by Yearling, an imprint of Random House Children's Books, a division of Penguin Random House LLC, New York. Originally published in hardcover in the United States by Delacorte Press, an imprint of Random House Children's Books, New York, in 2015.

Yearling and the jumping horse design are registered trademarks of Penguin Random House LLC.

Visit us on the Web! randomhousekids.com

Educators and librarians, for a variety of teaching tools, visit us at RHTeachersLibrarians.com

The Library of Congress has cataloged the hardcover edition of this work as follows:
Kelly, Katy.
Melonhead and the later gator plan / by Katy Kelly ; illustrated by Gillian Johnson.
pages cm
Summary: While visiting his grandparents' retirement community in Florida, ten-year-old Adam "Melonhead" Melon, accompanied by his best friend, Sam, invents the Alligator Distractor.
ISBN 978-0-385-74166-8 (hardcover) — ISBN 978-0-375-98669-7 (ebook)
[1. Florida—Fiction. 2. Grandparents—Fiction. 3. Retirement communities—Fiction.
4. Behavior—Fiction. 5. Friendship—Fiction. 6. Humorous stories.] I. Johnson, Gillian, illustrator. II. Title.
PZ7.K29637Mgi 2015
[Fic]—dc23
2013048814

ISBN 978-0-307-92971-6 (pbk.)

Printed in the United States of America

10 9 8 7 6 5 4 3 2 1

First Yearling Edition 2016

To my genius editor, Beverly Horowitz, who is generous and wise, kind and rich in good ideas. All writers should be so lucky.

1

WOW

I sat on my mom's suitcase so she could yank the zipper closed.

"It's five-thirty in the morning," I said. "It's almost time for WOW."

She looked at me.

"WOW stands for Week of Wonders," I said.

"But I won't be here," she said.

"That's why it's a WOW," I said. "It's the first time in history that I'll be living without a lady around. And by lady, I mean you, Mom."

"Thank you," she said.

"But I'm wondering what the Wonders are. And why you can't have them when I'm home."

"I can't reveal the WOW list," I said. "Sam and I are in a pact. You can't break a pact with your top friend."

"Now I'm worried," my mom said.

"You should be thrilled," I told her. "Believe me. I know what I'm talking about."

That's because I'm the one who came up with the WOW List of Manly Things for Sam and Me to Do with Dad While Mom's in Vermont with Her Sister and Lady Cousins. Sam decided the list should count down from Important to Extremely Important to Most Important Thing in the World.

5. Burping contest.
4. Cook chili with Tabasco, cayenne, and
   jalapeños. Eat it.
3. Ride to both ends of every subway line
   in Washington, D.C.
2. Drill holes in wood.
1. Adopt a dog.

Whenever I ask my mom if I can get a dog, she says, "You're not old enough."

And I always say, "If I were old enough, I'd pick a huge, furry dog that has a load of energy and likes to roll in mud." Then she makes a sound like she's shivering.

Last week, I had a double Brainflash of Brilliance.

1. I realized who is old enough: my mom.
2. My kind of dog is not my mom's kind of dog. Her kind is a mini dog that wears ear bows and doesn't cause allergies.

That's fine with me. My motto is Every Dog Is a Great Dog. As long as there's a dog living in my house, I'm happy.

I was going hyper from wanting to tell my mom the exciting news that she was getting a pet. I made myself wait until my dad got home so he wouldn't be the last one to know.

He walked in carrying a box from Baking Divas.

"Surprise!" he said. "I brought Plum Perfect Pudding."

My mom hugged his neck. "The best presents are the ones I wouldn't buy for myself," she said. "My favorite surprises are the ones the whole family can enjoy."

A dog is exactly that kind of surprise, I thought. *Wait until she comes home from her trip and finds out we got her a dog she wouldn't buy for herself.*

So even though I could hardly stand it, I kept the secret. Except I told Sam, of course.

"I'll carry your suitcase downstairs, Mom," I said.

"It's too heavy for you," she said.

"No, it's not," I said. "It's light."

My mom gave me the look that means "Don't argue."

"It rolls," I said. "I'll push it like a lawn mower."

That was a great idea, except Sam rang the doorbell when I was halfway down the steps. I tried to get in front of the suitcase. That didn't work as well as you'd think.

My dad opened the door while I picked up myself and the suitcase.

"Hey, Mrs. Melon," Sam yelled. "Your taxi's here!"

4

"I'll get the rest of your stuff, Betty," my dad yelled up the stairs.

"The second your mom leaves, we have to go to the pound," Sam told me.

"Before they're out of dogs," I said.

"If you and your dad don't pick the same dog, I'll be on your side," Sam said. "I'm great at convincing."

True. Sam convinced his mom to let him spend Fall Break with my Dad and me here in Washington, D.C., instead of with his toddler cousins in Philadelphia. Mrs. Alswang has to go because her niece, Sophia, had an unexpected baby. Well, she did expect it, but she thought it would get here in November instead of yesterday afternoon. Sophia's husband is in Peru with Sam's dad, taking pictures for *National Geographic*. Somebody has to help with all those children, so Mrs. Alswang and Sam's sister, Julia, are going to Philadelphia this morning, right after rush hour. I doubt Julia will be much help. One-year-olds usually aren't.

The taxi driver honked.

Sam and I dragged the suitcase down to the sidewalk. My dad rushed down the steps carrying more bags. The driver was shoving my mom's rolling suitcase into the trunk when my mother came out, walking an inch a minute so the plastic cake carrier in her arms wouldn't tip.

"Ready, Betty?" my dad asked.

"Hop into the cab, Mom," I said.

My mother did not hop. She stood like her feet were cemented to the sidewalk.

"I've come to my senses," she said.

My dad pushed a plaid tote bag across the taxi's backseat.

"What did you say, Betty?"

"I'm not going," she said.

"You have to go," Sam said. "You have a ticket."

"You'll have fun," my dad said.

"Vermont's too far away," she said.

"You can call us," my dad said.

"From the train," she said. "But there's no phone reception at the cabin. What if DB needs me?"

DB is my compromise name. It's short for Darling Boy, which is what my mom called me until this year, when I turned ten. Her second choice is Adam. My only choice is Melonhead.

My mom blames my friend Lucy Rose Reilly for inventing that nickname. I still thank her. Lucy Rose. Not my mom. Well, sometimes I thank my mom, but not for thinking Darling Boy is a good nickname.

"You can email us, honey," my dad said.

"My sister will understand," she said.

"No, she won't," I said. "Aunt Traci says the trip's the only reason she agreed to turn forty."

Supersonic brain-to-brain message to Sam: *Keep loading.*

"Here comes party food," I yelled. "Catch!"

Sam did. But a couple things jumped out midair. The French bread landed in a puddle near the curb.

"Don't worry, Mom!" I yelled. "Only one end is damp. The rest is mostly dry."

"I caught the olive jar right before it hit the street," Sam said.

"Unload the cab," my mom ordered. "I'm staying."

"Honey, you've been planning this trip since your sister's last birthday," my dad said.

"I can't leave for four days," she said. "The boys could get into a situation."

"They get in situations when you're here," my dad said.

"That's true," I said.

"Lots of them," Sam added.

"The meter's running, lady," the driver yelled out the window. "Are you coming?"

"What if the boys climb on the roof again?" my mom said.

"We're over that," I told her.

"Sometimes I'm tempted," Sam said.

"Sam," my dad said, "can we discuss your temptation after Mrs. Melon is on her way?"

"Sure," Sam said. "If you want to."

My dad kissed my mom's forehead and said, "We'll be fine, Betty. Go. Have a great time."

She got in the taxi, but she didn't shut the door.

"Go to bed on time," my mom said in her boss voice. "Remember the Polite People Program."

My mother invented 3P after she saw me licking my knife at Joshua Stern's bar mitzvah lunch. I only did it because a clump of mayonnaise was on it.

"We love you," my dad said. "Don't we, Sport?"

"Yep," I said.

He closed the car door. My mom kissed me through the open window.

She was nervous. I could tell from her breathing.

"What will you do if you need me, DB?"

I know how to relax her mind.

"I don't need you at all," I said.

For no reason, my dad gave me an XLG. The Xtreme Laser Glare—the worst of the glares.

2

THE SIXTEEN-STEP SECRET

"Men," my dad said. "It's eight a.m. The train has left the station. WOW has officially begun."

"Get the car keys, Dad!" I shouted. "And get ready for WOW number one!"

"Hold on, Sport," he said. "The Official WOW Opening Activity is the Bachelors' Breakfast. Tell me about WOW One while we're cooking. OK?"

"To the kitchen!" Sam shouted.

"Don't kick the swinging door," my dad said.

"I'll remember next time," I promised.

My dad let us sit on the counter. That's called a rare privilege. My mom thinks counter-sitting germs up the food.

"Is the Official Breakfast eggs?" Sam asked.

"Eggs are for the faint-hearted," my dad said.

"Toast?" I guessed.

He snorted. "Toast is for the timid," he said.

"Bacon?" I asked.

"Bacon is a preferred bachelor food," my father said.

He opened the fridge and pulled out a white shopping bag.

"Gentlemen," he said. "Since the beginning of time, the Sixteen Secret Steps of the Bachelor's Breakfast have been passed from father to son. Or, in Sam's case, from best friend's father to best friend."

"We enjoy Secret Steps," I said.

"Every man assembles his own Bachelor Breakfast," he said. "But I'll cook the main ingredient."

"Hot diggity dog," I said.

"You are correct," my dad said. "These will be the hot-diggity-est dogs ever created."

"Hot dogs?" Sam said. "For breakfast? For real?"

My dad reached into the bag.

"Step one: dogs on the griddle," he said.

"What's step two?" Sam asked.

"Steps two and three: open rolls, apply butter," my dad said. "Step four: put rolls facedown on the griddle."

According to my mom, Sam and I aren't allowed to griddle.

"When the rolls are golden, fill them with shredded cheese," my father said. "That's step five."

"It's getting better," Sam said.

"Step six: put a dog in the roll," he said.

"It's melting the cheese," I said.

My dad got a bowl. "Steps seven, eight, nine, ten, and eleven: mix ketchup, mustard, mayo, relish, and Tabasco to make Bachelor Sauce," he said.

"What's step twelve?" I asked.

"Pickles on the right bun. Step thirteen: banana peppers, on the left."

"I thought thirteen would be sauerkraut," Sam said.

"Sauerkraut is step fifteen," my dad said. "Step fourteen is smother with chili."

"What's sixteen?" I asked.

"Bacon," my dad said. "Of course."

"This is the best thing I ever ate," I said.

"I know," my dad said.

For entertainment, I said it again in burpspeak.

Burpspeaking is one of my top skills. It's E-Z. Just catch the burp on the way up your throat and say a word at the same time the burp's coming out of your mouth. Some words burp better than others.

"Let's keep that remarkable talent between us men," my dad said.

"Is it time to hear my plan, Dad?"

"Ready and listening," he said.

"You know how Mom goes ape over surprises?" I said.

"I do know," my dad said.

His phone started playing "Yankee Doodle."

"Don't answer!" I shouted.

"It's a phone, not a disaster," Sam said.

"You're wrong," I said. "When the phone plays 'Yankee Doodle,' it means my dad's boss is calling."

"Hello, Congressman," my dad said.

Then he asked, "How many points?"

Sam gave me a thumbs-up. "Points are good."

"In politics, points go up and down," I said. "Congressman Buddy Boyd doesn't call when they're up."

"So Buddy Boyd's behind?" Sam asked.

That made me hoot.

When Sam realized what he said, he fell apart laughing.

My dad gave us an XLG with daggers on top.

"Sir," he said, "if you want to win this election, you've got to get on the next plane to Tallahassee. Defend yourself. . . .

"I can't go to Florida right now, sir. Betty's out of town. I'm taking care of our son and his best friend."

I don't know what Congressman Buddy Boyd said, but my dad answered, "I can't do that, sir. They're only ten."

Then came the worst words.

"You fly down now, Congressman," my dad said. "I'll follow as soon as I can rearrange things."

My cheeks turned red hot.

"WOW is canceled, isn't it?" I said.

"I'm sorry, Sport," my dad said. "I wanted to spend Fall Break with you boys."

"That's OK," Sam said.

"No it's not," I said.

"Tell me about your surprise for Mom," he said.

"The Congressman ruined it," I said.

"Can we postpone it?" my dad asked.

"It has to happen while Mom's away," I said.

"Starting this minute," Sam said. "It takes days to get a dog. They have to inspect your family."

My dad laughed so hard his eyes crunched shut. "Mom feels you're not old enough to have a puppy," he reminded me.

"It's not for me," I said. "It's for Mom."

"Mrs. Melon's old enough to get five dogs," Sam said.

"Sport, you know Mom's reasons for not wanting a dog," my dad said.

"They bring dirt in the house, chew furniture, get fleas, jump on people, and slobber on everything," I said. "Plus what if it bites me and I get a scar?"

"You like scars," Sam said.

"Everybody does except my mom," I said.

"What made you think Mom would like a dog?" my dad asked.

"The Melon Family Guideline for Life," I explained. "The one that says Think of Others. I thought of Mom. I figured out that when she says no dog, she means she doesn't want a boy dog."

"A male dog?" my dad asked.

"A dog that likes to do what boys like to do," Sam said. "Run free and dig holes. Mrs. Melon would love a mom dog."

"A mom dog?" my dad asked.

"The ultra-small, calm kind of dog that gets haircuts and rides around in a dog purse," I said. "And

I'm OK with that. I'll feed it and walk it for Mom. But I'm taking the ear bows off before I take him outside."

"When Melonhead wants to hang around with a boy's dog, he can visit my dog," Sam said. "When I get it."

"You're getting a dog?" my dad asked Sam.

"After I show responsibility and commitment," Sam said.

"Commitment means earning fifty dollars to help pay for it," I said.

"Aren't pound puppies free?" my dad asked.

"Sure, but you have to pay for dog health," Sam said.

"You have fifty dollars, Dad," I said. "And Mom has responsibility."

My dad hugged me.

"I'm sorry, Sport. We cannot spring a dog on your mom. It's not fair to her or the dog."

"This is officially the worst Fall Break in the history of life," I said.

3

I MIGHT AS WELL BE AT SCHOOL

Sam ate my leftover Bachelor Breakfast.

"I'm too mad to eat," I told my dad.

"I understand," he said.

"How could you?" I asked. "Did your father ever cancel WOW weekend?"

It was a trick question. WOW weekend didn't exist back then, because I hadn't been born to invent it.

"I'm sorry, Sport," he said.

Then he asked Sam, "When's your dad getting home?"

"Not until he and Oliver find a yellow-tailed woolly monkey," Sam said. "That could be weeks, because they're endangered."

"The monkeys, not the men," I said.

I used my rude voice so he'd know I wasn't over being mad.

"I'll call Madam and Pop," my dad said.

Pop and Madam are our friends. Also Lucy Rose's grandparents. And the backup to the backup plan.

"They're in Louisiana," Sam said.

"The disappointments keep piling up," I said.

"For Madam and Pop too," Sam said. "They'll be ultra sad when they hear they missed their chance to have us at their house for five days."

"Time for Plan C," my dad said.

"What's that?" I asked.

"I'll let you know when I think of it, Sport," he said. "But throw some clothes in your backpack. And, Sam, if you unpacked your backpack, repack it."

Sam and I wear the same thing every day: cargo shorts, T-shirts, high-top sneakers, and Washington Nationals baseball caps. We've got never-ending Nattitude.

"My other shorts are in the laundry," I said.

"Bathing suits are shorts with built-in under-wear," Sam said.

I dug to the bottom of the clothes hamper and found damp swim trunks and three T-shirts that didn't smell too bad. I stuffed all that and clean underwear in my knapsack with zero folding.

When we came downstairs, my dad and his suitcase were on the front porch.

"Great news," he said. "I caught Sam's mom before she and Julia left town. They're driving over."

Sam looked like he got swacked in the face with a wet sock.

"To pick me up?" Sam asked.

"To bring you extra clothes," my dad said.

"Why?" I asked.

"You'll need them in Paradise."

"I've always wanted to go to Paradise!" Sam shouted.

"Ditto," I said. "Where is it?"

"Florida," my dad said.

"Is this a joke?" I asked.

"No," my dad said.

I somersaulted into my victory dance.

"Are we staying with Nana and Jeep?" I shouted.

I used to call my grandfather GP. That shortcut turned into Jeep. Nana's always been called Nana. Probably because lots of grandmas are.

"This is the best idea since air horns," I said.

"This is WOW times infinity," Sam said.

"Florida is more exciting than you are, Dad," I said. "No offense."

"There's my mom," Sam said.

"Get in the car!" Mrs. Alswang yelled. "Julia and I are driving you to the airport."

"Belwenhed n Sssams!" Julia said when we climbed in the backseat. To be friendly, she licked my eyebrow and threw diaper wipes at Sam.

"Tell me about Paradise," Mrs. Alswang said to my dad.

"I haven't seen it," my dad said. "My parents moved there a couple months ago. It's in St. Augustine. It's a community for people sixty and older."

The air went out of me.

"Dad! Nobody will believe Sam and I are sixty! We're too short."

"To sort," Julia said.

"Kids can visit," my dad said.

"I called your mom," Mrs. Alswang told my dad. "I was afraid two boys would be too much responsibility."

"Jeep and Nana are responsible, right, Dad?"

"I'd say my parents are responsible."

"You have to be if you collect blood," I said.

"Weird but interesting hobby," Sam said.

I could see Mrs. Alswang's eyeballs in the mirror. They were practically popping.

"My folks work for the Red Cross a couple half days a week," my father explained. "Dad drives the Bloodmobile. Mom's a nurse. When they're working, the boys can do activities at the clubhouse."

"There's a clubhouse?" I said. "With butlers? Do they wear tuxedos?"

"Do they say, 'Very good, sir'?" Sam asked. "They do in movies."

"I think this clubhouse is more like the YMCA," my dad said.

"The Y is swank," I said. "It has vending machines and a pool."

"Apool," Julia said.

"Please remember . . . you're guests in Paradise," Mrs. Alswang said. "I'll be mortified if you get into a situation."

"Zero incidents. Zero situations," Sam said. "It won't be like last week."

"Don't worry, Linda," my dad said. "I have two brothers, no sisters. My parents understand the ways of boys, right down to their unwashed socks."

Supersonic brain-to-brain message to Sam: *How does my dad know about our socks?*

4

PIT STOP

"We've got time for a two-minute stop at Baking Divas," Mrs. Alswang said.

"To get us snacks for the plane?" I asked.

"To get a present for Jeep and Nana," Mrs. Alswang said. "Charge it to our account, Sam."

"I'll go with him," I said. "For added speed."

Our friends Jonique, Pip, and Lucy Rose were at the worktable putting sugar eyeballs on Wiggly Piggly cupcakes. When they saw us, they raced to the front.

Lucy Rose and Jonique stood on boxes and leaned over the top of the glass case. Pip rolled over to the cash-register counter.

"My mom's paying us to work two hours a day," Jonique said. Her mom's a Diva.

"We're going to be rolling in riches and lolling in loot," Lucy Rose said. "Are you green from envy?"

"Nope," I said. "We're going to Florida."

"You're making that up," Pip said.

"Go ask my dad," I said. "After we buy a cake for my grandparents, it's adios, girls. Bonjour, airport."

"I'm green as lime Jell-O," Lucy Rose said.

"Lincoln Logs travel well," Mrs. McBee said.

She meant the cookie, not the toy. Because what would my grandparents want with wooden sticks?

Sam picked Pound for Pound Cake.

Pip tied red-and-white string around the box. Then she pulled up her backsack that hangs on her wheelchair. She fished out a dollar.

"Here," she said. "It's from my mom for carrying her groceries. I keep forgetting to give it to you."

"I told her not to pay," Sam said. "Due to what happened to the eggs."

"She said to put it in your dog fund," Pip said.

"Thanks," Sam said. "Only forty-three bucks and ninety-two cents to go."

"All you have is six dollars and eight cents?" Jonique said. She has math talent.

"He had more," I said. "We had to give up twenty dollars because of the situation with Mrs. Lee's porch light."

"Your mom's beeping the horn," Mrs. McBee said.

"Keep in touch with us from Florida," Pip said.

"I'm sure Jeep and Nana will let us use their phone to text you," I said.

"Mom, can they use your phone number if they want to text us?" Jonique asked.

Mrs. McBee nodded and gave us her number and her email, just in case.

"And you know my email and Sam's," I said. "Since you're at Baking Divas so much, we'll send your emails here. Then you can all read them at the same time."

5

VIPs

Julia spent the ride to Reagan National Airport pinching my nose. Sam spent the whole time laughing.

"Ow," Julia said for me. "Ow, nos."

Mrs. Alswang parked in the short-term lot and got in line with us.

"This is my second plane ride," Sam said. "The first one was when I was three months old. I don't remember that much about it."

"We have three seats on the noon flight," the ticket man said. "Two together. One in the last row."

"You can have the lonely one, Dad," I said.

Mrs. Alswang hugged Sam so tight she practically strangled his body.

"Be on your best behavior," she told him. "Mind your manners."

"E-Z P-Z, nice and pleasy," Sam said. "Thanks to Melonhead's mom and 3P, we have way more manners than we can use."

"Canoes," Julia said.

"Here's some gum," Mrs. Alswang said. "Chew it if you feel pressure in your ears."

My ears fly fine, but I never turn down a gum opportunity.

We were allowed to get on early with the traveling-with-children people. The flight attendant showed us 18A and 18B. I gave Sam 18A. It was a window seat.

Her badge said OLIVIA LAVIE.

"Do we call you Olivia or Ms. Lavie?" I asked.

My mom says kids can't call adults by their first names unless the adult says it's OK. It's a 3P thing.

"Olivia is fine," she said. "If you need anything during the flight, press the button. I'll come."

Sam smiled. "We have a personal flight attendant."

"Are we VIPs?" I asked.

"All my passengers are very important," Olivia said. "But kids twelve and under get extra attention."

She gave us plastic pilot wings.

"We're too mature for these," Sam said. "But I'll keep mine in case I meet a young child."

"I'm putting mine on my Wall of Memories," I said.

Thirty seconds after Olivia left, Sam pushed the button. She was back in a flash.

"Just testing," Sam said.

Sam and I held our breath until the plane got over the clouds. Lucy Rose says you have to if you want luck.

I pushed the overhead button. No one came until the pilot announced, "You're free to walk around the cabin."

"Is there an emergency?" Olivia asked.

"A big one," I said. "Those people didn't pay attention to your oxygen mask warning."

"Do you want us to explain the emergency directions to them?" Sam asked.

"That's OK," Olivia said.

She left. I pushed the button.

"Did you mean 'It's OK, explain safety to them' or 'It's OK that they didn't listen'?" I asked.

"I meant 'It's OK, don't worry about it,'" she said.

I called her back.

"Where's the cabin?" I asked. "The one we're free to walk around in."

"The cabin is the inside of the plane," she said. "But I'd appreciate it if you didn't walk around unless you have to use the bathroom."

"One more question," I said. "When you flush the toilet on a plane, does the water go into the air?"

"No," she said.

"Good," Sam said. "That would be gross."

Sam did a long drum solo on his seat-back tray. I found a ballpoint pen in the seat pocket in front of me. I drew dog faces on my palms. I'm trying to be ambidextrous. The left dog looked like a hedgehog.

I left-handedly pushed the silver button on my armrest.

BAM!

My seat flopped back fast. I was staring up a man's nostrils.

Supersonic brain-to-brain message to Sam: *Whoa, Beau! This guy has a load of nose hair.*

"Your seat is in my lap," Mr. Nose Hair said.

1. That was an exaggeration of three or more inches.
2. He was reading close to my scalp, which I'm pretty sure is rude.

Luckily, I remembered my mom's motto Look People in Their Eyes. I locked my eyeballs on his and waited for him to talk. He said, "Would you mind putting your seat in the upright position?"

"I don't mind," I said.

It didn't bounce back to upright position. This time the man pushed the overhead button.

After Olivia fixed my seat, she said, "Don't touch the seat button anymore."

"When is it going to be time for pretzels?" Sam said.

"I'll bring them with the beverage service," Olivia said.

"We're bonkers for beverages," I said in my cartoon voice.

"Do kids get served first?" Sam asked.

"Can we have all the snacks we want?" I asked.

"Can you estimate how many minutes until beverages come?" Sam asked.

Guess what Olivia did? She got two Coca-Colas and four packs of pretzels and gave them to us. Everybody else had to wait.

"VIP is the life for me," I said.

Olivia tapped the mini TV screens on the seats in front of us with her long fingernail. An alligator appeared. "You'll enjoy this TV program about Florida," she said.

"She sounds like she has a headache," Sam said.

"Probably caused by bothersome passengers," I said.

6
ALLIGATOR EGGS

The airplane TV showed a lady in a doctor coat.

"Welcome to *Florida: Nature's Wonderland*," she said. "I'm veterinarian Dr. Judith Garcia. We're at Jack's Reptile Farm with first grader Tuan Phan."

"Hotpachonga!" Sam said. "I never knew there was such a thing as a reptile farm."

The TV showed Tuan Phan's big blue rubber gloves. He was holding a white egg.

"It looks ready to hatch," Dr. Garcia told Tuan Phan.

"The shell's soft," Tuan Phan said. "I can feel the alligator moving inside."

"There's a tear in the shell," Dr. Garcia said.

"I didn't do it," Tuan Phan said.

"The alligator did," Dr. Garcia said.

"Here comes a nose!" Sam said.

"Oh, my sweet beet," I shouted. "It's smiling!"

"Tuan Phan, you can help it hatch by tearing the shell," Dr. Garcia said. "It's safe. Alligators are born without teeth."

"Its front feet look like baby alien hands," Sam said.

"Who knew baby alligators are striped?" I said.

"By the 1960s the American alligator was so scarce it became a protected animal," Dr. Garcia said. "They came back in a big way. Today there are over one million wild alligators in Florida. That's one alligator for every nineteen people."

"Florida is one lucky state, mate," I said.

"And the population is growing," Dr. Garcia said. "Female alligators lay between thirty and fifty eggs at a time. We call that a clutch. In the wild, most eggs get eaten by birds, raccoons, snakes, bobcats, otters, and sometimes other alligators."

"That's terrible," Sam said.

Dr. Garcia pointed at a pool filled with alligators.

"Kids are throwing marshmallows at them!" Sam said.

"They're as long as my dad's legs," I said. "Not the marshmallows. The alligators."

"How did they teach them to catch with their mouths?" Sam asked.

"It's like training a dog," I said. "I bet they start with baby alligators and baby marshmallows."

A big gator made a splashy U-turn to eat a marshmallow before the little guys could get to it.

"Alligators have a fondness for marshmallows," Dr. Garcia said. "But the truth is these reptiles aren't picky eaters. They've been known to swallow spark plugs, rocks, and pop bottles."

I hooted.

Dr. Garcia picked up a baby gator. "If you'd like to see alligators up close and personally, Florida has many reptile farms that offer tours," she said. "Depending on where you are in Florida, you might spot a wild alligator. If you do, give it space. You wouldn't like it if one walked into your house. They don't like it when you walk into theirs."

"I'd love it if one walked into my house," I said.

"Ditto," Sam said.

"I'd buy it a red leash and take it for walks around the neighborhood," I said.

"I'd let it swim in our laundry-room sink," Sam said.

"If there was no such thing as dogs, the best pet would be a baby alligator," I said.

"Absolutely," Sam said.

7

THE VILLA

Sam was out-of-his-head excited to be in Florida.

We'd been driving for six minutes when my dad said, "Sam, if you are going to scream 'Palm tree!' every time you see one, I'm going to turn the radio to the opera station."

Sam stopped.

"If we had a palm tree at home, I'd climb up and pick coconuts for breakfast," he said.

"Only coconut palms produce coconuts," my dad said.

"That's the kind I'd have," Sam said.

"Washington gets too cold for palms," I said. "They'd only survive inside."

Nana and Jeep were wait-
ing in the front yard.

"Helloooo!" Nana yelled.
To me, her voice sounds like
music.

Jeep had on his blue-
and-orange desert hat. It
has a flap that keeps his
neck from getting fried.
He was wearing plaid shorts,
a green shirt, all-color socks, and
sandals. Happy Socks are the only kind of socks he
wears.

Nana was wearing a light blue dress and white
sunglasses that made her look like an owl. In a good
way.

Sam handed over the box from Baking Divas.

"Well, aren't you the sweetest thing on two legs,"
Nana said.

"The cake's a little dented," Sam told her. "The
airplane rule is put it under your seat. I have the
habit of swinging my legs."

"Hello, Sam," Jeep said. "Welcome to Paradise."

Sam shook Jeep's hand. Then we all had a hug festival.

My father said, "I like the new house, Mom and Dad."

It's weird that parents have parents.

"They call the houses villas," Nana said in a fancy voice.

"Are all the villas tan?" I asked.

"No," Jeep said. "Some are light tan, some are medium tan, and some are dark tan."

"Melonhead and I will paint your villa any color you want," Sam said.

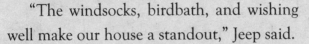

"I wouldn't ask you to do that," Nana said. "You're on vacation."

"We don't mind," I said.

"How do you remember which villa is yours?" Sam asked.

"The windsocks, birdbath, and wishing well make our house a standout," Jeep said.

"And the Miami Dolphins flag," Nana added. "And the pink flamingo wearing a miniature football helmet."

"It's not easy to dress a flamingo," Jeep said.

"I can tell who's the chief landscaper," my dad said.

"I've been trying to get your dad to focus on the backyard," Nana said. "I'd like the front to be less interesting."

"Son," Jeep said in a droopy voice, "your mother wants a white picket fence."

"A fence would look great," my dad said.

"I'm on Jeep's side," I said. "The more stuff, the better."

"Let me show you your room, boys," Nana said.

The walls were swimming-pool blue.

"I'm glad I'm here," Sam said.

Nana smiled. "I'm glad you're both here. Unpack. We're having lunch on the back deck."

It took a nanosecond to dump our backpacks on the floor.

"Which bed is mine?" Sam asked.

"I'm a guest, but you're the guest's guest," I said. "You get first pick."

"The one by the window."

I flipped into a handstand.

"Handwalk to the kitchen!" I called.

When we got there, we listened through the window. You would be amazed at what you can find out by eavesdropping.

"We've lived here two months," Nana was saying. "I thought we'd have made friends by now."

"Give the people a chance to discover us, Doll," Jeep said. "Once they do, we'll have to lock the doors to get a minute to ourselves."

"Most of our neighbors moved in ten years ago

when Paradise first opened," Nana said. "I feel like the new kid at school."

I handwalked out the sliding door.

"Oops, sorry, Dad," I said. "Did my foot hurt your neck?"

"Not much," he said. "But I'd like you to stand up before you whack Nana."

"I'd like that too," Nana said.

"Sam, please bring out the platter of BLTs," Nana said. "Adam, get five glasses, please."

"I'm allowed to carry glasses? Glasses made of glass?" I asked.

"Melonhead's mom doesn't let kids carry glass," Sam said.

"We all pitch in here," Jeep said. "House rule."

"Cool beans," I said.

"I'll get the avocados," Nana said. "Jeep, pour the limeades. Mike, round up plates, silverware, and napkins, please."

"Hey!" I said. "You have a river in your backyard!"

"It's a canal," Jeep said.

For a good view, I boosted myself onto the top of the deck railing.

"Let's go crabbing!" Sam shouted. "And fishing!"

"I've tried," Nana said. "No luck."

"Because the alligators eat them," I said.

"There are no alligators in Paradise," Nana said.

"Are you telling me that out of over a million alligators in Florida, not *one* is in this canal?" I said.

"Not one," Jeep said.

"That's unfair," Sam said.

"When they built Paradise, the developers put underwater steel mesh walls at both ends of the property," Jeep said. "Only water and small fish can get through."

"A baby alligator could," I said. "They're skinny. And slippery."

"Even the newly hatched ones are too big to slip through," Jeep said.

"That fence is against nature," I said. "Alligators have rights, you know."

"They also have teeth," Nana said. "Residents appreciate the underwater fence."

"They're afraid of getting eaten?" Sam asked.

"People eat more alligators than alligators eat people," Jeep said.

"People eat alligators?" I asked. "Hot diggity dog!"

"Hot diggity alligator," Jeep said.

"What do they taste like?" Sam asked.

"Alligator," Jeep said.

"Can we have it for dinner?" I said. "I want to write *Ate Alligator* on my Lifetime List of Achievements."

"Ditto," Sam said.

My dad laughed. "Thanks for taking the boys," he said. "They've promised to be responsible citizens."

"It won't be like when I was at your old house and I got my jeans caught in the ceiling fan," I said.

"We were grateful you weren't wearing them at the time," Nana said.

"I've gotten a load of maturity since then," I said.

"We haven't been in a situation in days," Sam said. "We're Thinking About Consequences."

"We're leaping before we look," I said.

"I hope you mean looking before you leap," Nana said.

"If that's how they do it in Florida, sign us up," Sam said.

"What's that about sinuses?" Jeep asked.

"Louder, boys," Nana said. "Jeep can't hear you."

"I can hear fine," Jeep said. "Most of the time."

"We'll yell when you're awake and whisper when you're napping," I said. "We know you're at the resting age."

"Says who?" Jeep asked.

"My mom," I said.

"Did she say why we need to rest?" Nana asked.

"Because you're old," I said.

"Sport!" my dad said. "Mom, I think what Betty meant was she didn't want the boys to be noisy because it's annoying."

Jeep and Nana laughed.

"I think what she meant was we're old," Nana said.

"I think that's what she meant too," Sam said.

"May I use your phone, Dad?" I asked. "I need to check if people are looking for me."

He handed it to me. "Absolutely. We all need friends," Dad said.

We used Mrs. McBee's number and sent a text to the girls so they'd have our number.

After lunch, Sam and I checked the phone.

> M & S, R U there yet? R U going swim-ming first thing? LR, J & P

I speed-typed the answer.

> LR, J & P, Yes. No, but soon. M & S

> M & S, Was it fun on the plane? J

> J, Fun times infinity. What's new with U? Has anything exciting happened at home? M & S

> M & S, One excellent thing is happen-ing. I'm not saying what it is. You will find out in your future. J

8

REMEMBER 3P

"Purple is a kingly color for a couch," Sam said.

"Thank you," Nana said. "Jeep picked it out."

"I'm going to call Betty," my dad said. "Any questions?"

"Betty called before you got here," Nana said. "We're up to date on the Melon Family Guidelines for Life and your house rules. Eat vegetables. Bed by nine. Wear sunscreen. No tying each other up. No juggling in the house. No experimenting with chemicals. No standing on furniture."

"Your mom said to remember 3P," Jeep said. "Do you know what that means?"

"Yes, but it's not as cinchy as it sounds," I said.

"It's the Polite People Program," Sam said. "Mrs. Melon invented it for Melonhead and me."

"Honey," my dad was saying, "the boys are safer here than on Capitol Hill. Paradise is car-free. Everyone walks, bikes, or drives a golf cart." Then he said, "No, they don't seem homesick. They seem thrilled."

"Thrilled to our gills!" I shouted.

My dad passed me the phone.

"Hi, Mom," I said.

"Were you scared on the plane?" she asked.

"I'm never scared on planes," I said.

"That's because you hold my hand during turbulence," she said.

"You grab my hand, Mom," I said. "To me turbulence is exciting."

"OK, DB. Remember to Think Before Acting," she said. "It prevents accidents."

"We don't have to think," I said. "If we get gashed or smashed or fall on our heads, Nana can fix us on the spot."

"Why would you get gashed or smashed?" my mom asked. "Or fall on your head?"

"No reason," I said.

"Use your manners," she said. "Be polite to Nana and Jeep's friends."

"They don't have any friends," I said.

"I hope Nana didn't hear you say that!"

"She already knows she's friendless," I said. "Who do you think told me?"

We walked my dad to the car.

"I'll call you, Sport," he said.

"I might be too busy to talk," I said. "But I'll report in every morning."

"We're lending the kids Jeep's phone," Nana told my dad. "He and I can share mine."

"I love you, Mom and Dad," my father said.

9
TANTOOS FOR TWO

Sam and I were inspecting the guest closet for cool stuff when Nana came in with towels.

"What are those for?" I asked.

"You might want to shower while you're here," she said.

"Doubt it," I said.

Nana laughed. "Put on sunblock, boys. We'll meet you in front of the garage."

Sam made a bowl with his hands. I squeezed the bottle.

"Brainflash of Brilliance!" I said.

"What's the BOB?"

"Tantoos," I said.

"Explain," Sam said.

I zipped across the hall and came back with Q-tips.

"Watch me," I said.

I dipped a Q-tip in Sam's dripping bowl-hands and started painting my cheek.

"You're missing a spot," Sam said.

"On purpose," I said. "When those places don't tan, I'll have lightning bolts on my cheeks."

"You're a one-of-a-kind mastermind!" Sam said, and grabbed a Q-tip.

"Oops," he said. "I forgot my hands are full of sunblock."

Luckily, SPF 50 blends into the carpet.

"Make my tantoo look like a bat landed on my face."

"Bottom half or top half?" I asked.

"The whole bat," he said.

"I mean top or bottom half of your face," I said.

"Top," Sam said. "So my eyes are in the middle of the wings."

"Do you want the bat to be tan or regular skin color?"

"Tan," he said.

Q-tips make excellent wing points.

"This is in the Cone of Silence," I said. "We don't want Nana and Jeep to notice our tantoos until they're worthy."

"Our faces are usually grubby," he said. "When our tantoos start showing, we'll add extra dirt."

"When we're outside without Nana and Jeep, we'll turn our baseball caps backwards and work on our tantoos," I said. "When we're with them, inside or outside, it is hats in forward position, heads down."

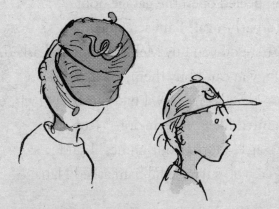

10
THE MELONMOBILE

"Who's ready to ride in the Mélonmobile?" Jeep asked.

"I was born ready!" I shouted.

"I don't even know what it is and I can't wait," Sam said.

Jeep peeled open the garage door.

"Hotpachonga!" Sam screamed.

"Where do you buy Melonmobiles?" I asked.

"Oh, you can't buy them," Nana said.

"For Nana's birthday, I had our boring white golf cart painted like a watermelon," Jeep said.

"It's an honor for our name," I said.

"Were you surprised?" Sam asked Nana.

"I was shocked," she said. "But I got used to it."

The outside of the Melonmobile was dark green with wiggly lime stripes.

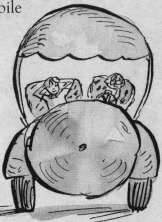

"The inside's like the inside of a watermelon," I said.

"The seeds were my idea," Jeep said.

"The back has the stub of a vine and fake leaves," Sam said. "Like it was picked."

"It's snazzy times infinity," I said. "How much did it cost?"

"The present giver never discusses the price of a gift in front of the present getter," Jeep said.

"Why not? I like knowing how much people pay for my gifts," I said. "It makes me feel valuable."

"Everyone is curious," Jeep said. "But it's rude to ask."

"I can't believe that's true," I said.

"And yet it is," Jeep replied.

11
THE P DE L

Nana sat in front with Jeep so Sam and I could ride on the backwards backseat. We like to see where we've been.

"I wish cars didn't have glass in the windows," Sam said.

"Who doesn't?" I said.

"Here's the community grove," Nana said. "We've got orange, lemon, lime, and key lime trees."

Jeep stopped under a row of trees.

"What's that racket?" I asked.

"Look up," Jeep said.

"Parrots!" Sam shouted. "Hundreds of parrots! A kingdom of parrots!"

"Stick out your arms and chirp," I said.

We stayed for ten minutes. Those birds had eight arms to land on. Not one came close. They didn't notice when we left.

"There are the tennis courts," Nana said.

"How much does it cost to play?" Sam asked.

"Nothing," Nana said. "Everything in Paradise is for the convenience of the residents."

"I like that deal," I said.

"And it's easy to find your way around," Jeep said. "In Paradise, all streets lead to the Ponce de León fountain. Or they lead to a street that leads to the Ponce de León fountain."

The P. de L is magnificent. Leaping dolphins are held up by hidden underwater pipes. Water rushes out of their mouths and rains on golden mermaids and mermen riding turtles. The turtles dribble into shells that are bigger than Jeep's birdbath. Ponce is on top. He has a sword.

"The only thing unrealistic is the baby alligators," Sam said. "I doubt they can climb straight up. They lack suction."

"If I owned a fountain I'd put myself on top," I said. "But I wouldn't be wearing ladies' boots."

"That was the fashion five hundred years ago," Nana said.

"Is Ponce famous?" Sam asked.

Nana nodded. "Everything in Paradise is named after a well-known Floridian."

"Why is Ponce known?" I asked.

"He was a Spanish explorer who docked his ship near St. Augustine in 1513," Jeep said. "He's also the first Floridian, because he named the land La Florida."

"I would have named it Melonheadia," I said.

"Or Samlandia," Sam said.

"I read that Ponce de León was searching for gold

and the Fountain of Youth," Nana said. "He'd heard the water could turn old people young."

"That's the fountain!" Sam said.

"Jump in, Nana and Jeep!" I yelled. "We can be kids together!"

"He didn't find gold or the Fountain of Youth," Nana said.

"This is the Fountain of People Over Sixty," Jeep said.

"I wish it worked," I told my grandparents.

The parking lot was at the bottom of a sloping hill.

"Rows and rows of plain white golf carts," I said. "And one perfect Melonmobile."

"We never have trouble finding this baby, do we, Doll?"

"It's impossible to lose," Nana agreed.

She put her arms around Sam's and my shoulders and steered us up the sloping sidewalk.

"Straight ahead is the Ponce de León Clubhouse," she said.

"Ponce gets a fountain and a building?" Sam asked.

"He's a Florida bigwig," Jeep said.

"Hey," I said. "They have parking in front."

"Those spaces are for the convenience of the residents who have trouble getting around," Jeep said. "The younger ones can walk from the lower lot."

"Where are the younger ones?" I asked.

"He means you and me," Sam said.

"He means us," Nana said.

"You're hilarious," I told her.

"First stop: the Ernest Hemingway Lounge," Jeep said.

"They have a room just for lounging?" Sam asked.

Nana laughed. "Most of the rooms are for activities. The Ernest Hemingway is where you go to relax, read, work a crossword puzzle. It's a quiet place you can make a phone call or use the computer."

"That's what I'm going to do," Sam said, looking at me.

When we got inside, Sam and I pulled chairs over to the computer. He typed. I dictated.

Dear Lucy Rose, Pip, and Jonique,

Paradise is paradise. We are writing from the Ponce de León Clubhouse, where everything is *For the Convenience of Residents.*

Residents are people who live here. Convenience means FREE.

What's the excellent thing you are doing?

Your friends,
Sam and Melonhead

P.S. We're getting tantoos on our faces. Tantoos are like tattoos, only better.

I wasn't sure my mom would see my message, but I sent it anyway.

Dear Mom,

We're at the Ponce. There was a bowl of chocolate Kisses on the table. The sign said Help Yourself.

Sam and I split them. Thirty for me. Thirty for him. We remembered you said don't ever take the last piece. I put one back.

Love,
Your son, Melonhead

P.S. I'm not living in a house.

She answered fast.

Darling B,

Just checking my email and I'm so happy to see one from you. What do you mean you're not living in a house? I hope you're not camping. The Florida mosquitoes will eat you alive. You have sensitive skin.

When I read that you helped yourself to thirty Kisses, I realized that you must have meant three. Try to type more carefully.

I'm trying to forget that you are 1,262 miles away from me.

Love,
Mom

Dear Mom,
    I'm living in a *villa*.
                    DB

P.S. Tell Aunt Traci I said happy
birthday!

"Move so I can write to my mom and sister," Sam
said.

Dear Mom,
    We are having fun. Tell Sophia a
good name for a baby is Ponce.
    Hope you get this.
                    Love,
                    Sam

Dear Sam,
    I was just about to write to you!
The new baby is adorable. No name
yet, but I doubt it will be Ponce.
I'll call when I get all the kids to
bed. We miss you.
                    Love,
                    Mom and Julia

We were about to leave when we got this:

Dear Sam and Melonhead,
    Are you nuts? Tattoos are the

worst idea you guys have ever had.
And you have had a lot of them.
                    Lucy Rose,
                    Jonique, and Pip

P.S. One hint about the EXCELLENT
thing we are doing: Mrs. McBee gave
us permission.

12

A SHOCK

I rolled myself into the hammock next to Jeep.

"Is it hard to fill in your sudoku while we're swinging?" I asked.

"Oddly enough, it is," Jeep said.

"You could sit in a chair," I said.

Sam came over and gave us a push and said, "Relax, Jeep. We can light the grill for you."

"No, you can't," Jeep said.

That was a disappointment.

Sam set the outside table. I got to cut a tomato. With a knife. I sliced it in half and cut the half in half. Then I cut the quarters in as many pieces as I could.

"I got carried away," I told Nana. "Maybe they won't want to eat it."

"Food sounds better in French," Nana said. "We'll call it *Morceaux de Tomates par la Tête de Melon.*"

"What's that mean?" Sam asked.

"Bits of Tomato by the Head of the Melon," Nana said.

That made me feel good.

After dinner Jeep said, "Root beer floats for dessert."

"Yabba-dabba-do, McGoo!" I yelled.

"My fave, Dave," Sam said.

Sam carried the ice cream to the table. Nana brought the root beer. Jeep scooped. I poured almost perfectly.

"Please pass me a straw," Nana said.

Sam reached over Jeep to give her one.

"Yowsa! That's cold!" Jeep shouted.

He had a float flood in his lap. Ice cream dripped down his leg.

"It was an accident," Sam said.

"I'd be alarmed if it was on purpose," Jeep said.

"I'll hose you off in the yard," Sam said.

"Problem solved," Jeep said.

Sam raced to the side of the house, turned on the faucet, and dragged the hose across the backyard.

He blasted Jeep's bottom half.

Jeep shook like a wet dog.

"Cold circulates the blood," Nana said.

"Then I'm as well circulated as a man wearing shorts in an igloo," Jeep said.

"Turn off the hose, Sam," Nana said. "Jeep, honey, put on dry clothes."

Sam dropped the hose and disappeared around the side of the villa.

"Other way, Sam!" I shouted.

"What?" Sam shouted.

"Turn the faucet the other way. The hose is like an out-of-control, water-shooting snake."

It blasted Nana. Her short gray hair looked like a mushroom hat.

"Grab the hose!" she yelled.

Sam and I ran for it. I slipped on the wet grass. Sam belly-flopped. We reached for the nozzle. Our heads bonked. I tipped into a yucca plant.

"It feels like I landed on spears!" I screamed.

"I've got the hose!" Sam yelled.

"Point the hose toward the canal, Sam!" Nana yelled.

Sam dropped the hose and screamed.

"Alligator!"

I bounced up.

"Where?"

"Near the tree!" Sam shouted. "See the tail?"

"Oh, my sweet potato," I said. "I bet it knows we ate its brother."

Fear made Sam drop the hose.

"I'm coming!" Jeep yelled.

His dry shorts got sprayed on the way.

"Come here!" Nana yelled. "All of you!"

"There's its tail!" Sam yelled.

"Where?" Jeep asked.

"It's going underwater," I said.

"It's going to pounce," Sam said. "I know it."

"It won't pounce," Jeep said.

"How do you know?" I asked.

"Because it's a tree root," Jeep said.

"Roots don't have green skin," Sam said.

"The green is algae," Jeep explained. "The water's moving. The root is not. It's an optical illusion."

Once Jeep said it was a root, I couldn't figure out how Sam made the mistake. But a top rule of friendship is never make your friend feel like a goofball.

"Anybody who saw it could be fooled," I said.

"When we tell people about this trip, can we leave this part out?" Sam asked.

"Of course."

It took me forever to type in all the names, but I only sent the email to Mom and Dad and Jonique. They could tell the others.

Dear Mom, Dad, Aunt Traci, Lady Cousins, Mrs. Alswang, Julia, Lucy Rose, Pip, and Jonique,

News flash!

From Melonhead: We ate alligator! Alligator meat is the color of pork chops. It has a smell. It tastes like chicken, in a swampy, greasy, chewy way. It turned Sam and me into burping machines. That's something we always wanted to invent.

From Sam: I do not recommend eating alligator, even for the burps.

P.S. From Melonhead to my dad:
1. Did the Congressman get any points yet?
2. You know what would improve alligator? Bachelor Sauce.

P.S. From Sam to my mom and Julia: How's Philadelphia? Remind Julia about me.

P.S. To the Girls: Is the thing you're doing excellent or EXCELLENT?

We got answered pretty quick.

Dear Melonhead and Sam,
    It's me, Pip. Jonique and Lucy

Rose feel disgusted that you ate alligator.

I feel like you have courage. I
ate octopus once.

The surprise is SO EXCELLENT IT'S
STUPENDOUS.

Your friend,
Pip

P.S. Mrs. McBee tried a new recipe
invention: Banana Pockets. Jonique
thinks they're P-U, but she hates
bananas.

P.P.S. Lucy Rose thinks it would
be polite if you bring us a gift,
please. She says that's what Madame
and Pop do when they go away.

13

TOM SWIFT, BOY INVENTOR

Nana is the worst at
Pictionary. Everything
she draws looks like a
frying pan or a frying
pan with legs.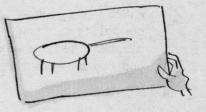

Jeep and Sam won three times in a row.

"Rematch," I said.

"It's teeth-brushing time," Nana said.

"That's a seven-second job," I said.

"Zero seconds for me," Sam said. "I forgot my
toothbrush."

"Ditto," I said. "But it's OK. We're only here for
a couple of days."

"New toothbrushes are in the linen closet," Nana said.

I hugged her goodnight.

"Nana," I said, "don't worry about getting friends. I was the new kid at school once. It works out."

I brushed fast. Then I smeared lemon soap on my cheeks and dunked my head in the bathroom sink. It overflowed. Sam and I mopped it up with two rolls of toilet paper.

"Why are you washing your face?" Sam asked.

Normally we don't. It's a waste of time and soap.

"Tantoo inspection," I said.

"Oh, I forgot I was getting one," Sam said.

I looked in the shell mirror.

"Faint but fine, Pal of Mine!" Sam said.

"Wash and dunk, Skunk," I said.

When Sam came up for air, I could see a faint outline of tan wings. "You're getting batified," I said.

We were in our beds when Jeep came in. I yanked my sheets up to eyeball level to hide my tantoo. Sam covered his cheeks with his hands.

"Would you young genius inventors like me to

read you a book about another young genius inventor?" Jeep asked.

"Sure," I said.

"Ditto," Sam said.

"*'Tom Swift and His Photo Telephone,'*" Jeep read.

I hooted.

"Tom's not swift," I said. "Philippe Kahn invented the camera phone in 1997."

"This book was written in 1914," Jeep said.

"How did the author know the future?" I asked.

Tom Swift is a lot like Sam and me. Except we don't call cars automobiles.

14

WILD DOGS

I shook Sam awake.

"Listen!" I shouted.

"Dogs?" he mumbled.

"Packs of dogs," I said.

Sam yawned. "Dogs come in packs?"

"They sound like puppies," I said.

That got his brain moving.

"They sound scared," Sam said. "And hungry."

"It's up to us to rescue them," I said.

Sam pressed his face against the window screen.
"It's too dark to see them."

We ran down the hall. I threw open Nana and
Jeep's door. Sam flipped on the light.

"Emergency!" we screamed.

"Who's hurt?" Nana yelled.

Jeep jumped up in his T-shirt and boxers.

"We need flashlights," I said. "And leashes."

"Hurry!" Sam said. "Those dogs need us."

"I've never heard this much barking," I said.

"We have," Jeep said. "Every night."

"You shock me," I said. "Help Others is a Melon Family Guideline for Life. You're a Melon. Those dogs need help."

"Poor, sad dogs," Sam said.

"They're not sad dogs," Jeep said. "They're tree frogs."

"Barking tree frogs," Nana said.

"That can't be," I said.

"It can be, and it is," Jeep said.

"Seriously?" Sam asked.

"If I were a watchdog who wanted the night off, I'd hire a barking tree frog to fill in for me," Jeep said.

We all went outside and stood on the deck, shining flashlights on trees.

"Barking tree frogs are hard to spot," Jeep said. "They're hardly longer than my index finger."

"They come in different colors—brown, bright green, yellow, gray. They're spotted," Nana said.

"Blending with nature," I said. "That's smart."

"A barking tree frog would get me ready for a real dog," Sam said.

"I can't imagine how," Nana said.

"I can," I said. "We'll catch one in the morning."

"They're nocturnal," Jeep said. "Up at night. Asleep by day, like owls."

"So what you're saying is, start searching now," I said.

"That's *not* what I'm saying," Jeep said.

"In the dark, you might confuse a barking tree frog with a Cuban tree frog," Nana said.

"Cuban tree frogs are bigger and not as good-looking," Jeep said. "You don't want to accidentally grab one."

"Actually," Sam said, "we'd like any frog."

"Cuban tree frogs secrete toxic mucus from their skin," Nana said.

"Poison snot?" I said.

"That's another way to say it," Jeep said.

I hooted my head off. "Man-o-man! I wish I could ooze poison snot."

"Ditto times infinity," Sam said.

"Good night," Nana said in a firm voice.

15

FIRST THING IN THE MORNING

Sam woke me up by pounding my face with a starfish pillow. I faked sleep until he pushed up my eyelids with his thumbs. Then BAM! My pillow. His head.

"I am your Supreme Leader," I said in my alien voice.

Sam smacked my guts with the starfish. "I'm the Supreme Leader of the Supreme Leader!" he yelled.

"Good morning, Supreme Leaders," Jeep said. "Get dressed. Slather on sunblock. Nana needs oranges."

It took half a nanosecond to jump into yesterday's clothes. Outlining tantoos with Q-tips takes some minutes.

Nana was in the kitchen watching the coffeepot.

"Are you tired?" I asked. "Your face looks droopy."

"I am and it is," she said.

"We'll need money for oranges," I said.

"Fruit's free in Paradise," Jeep said.

"Everything's free in Paradise," Sam said. "I wish Capitol Hill had that deal. I'd set up an orange stand. When I collected fifty dollars I'd get a dog."

"I'd help you," I said.

"What kind of dog?" Nana asked.

"Any kind that sleeps in my bed at night and licks me when I come home from school," Sam said.

"I'll never get a dog in this childhood," I said.

Nana ruffled my hair. "No one gets everything, sweetie."

"Check in with your father," Nana said. "Then go pick a dozen oranges."

She handed me the phone.

```
Dad. In Paradise 19 hours. Zero situ-
ations. Adventure later. N & J say
hi. Luv, ur son
```

I passed the phone to Sam.

```
M & J, Any news from Dad? Sam
```

Just as Sam was handing the phone back to me, he heard a beep.

```
M & S, 2 help u guess what we r doing,
u can have 3 guesses. LR, J & P
```

16

ONE MAN'S GARBAGE

We took the long way to the grove so we could chase the trash truck. The truck stopped.

"Hey, mister!" I yelled. "Can we stand on the back and ride?"

The trash collector jumped off. According to his shirt, his name was Bobby.

He picked up the recycle can like it was air.

"You have to be eighteen to ride on a government vehicle," Bobby said.

The truck lifted, flipped, dumped, and gave the can back to Bobby. It's part truck, part robot.

"We have to walk all the way to the grove," Sam said.

"All the way is two blocks," Bobby said.

He tossed in a table that was down to three legs. The busted-off leg landed straight up like the sword of Camelot. Watching it get crushed to splinters, we nearly missed the treasure.

Bobby had his arms up, in the throwing position.

Sam and I screamed in one king-sized voice, "Don't!"

"We need that!" I said.

"For transportation," Sam said.

"My dad has that exact model," I said.

Bobby studied it, then set it back down.

"The wheels are in good shape," he said.

"The lever works," I said.

"Drive safely," Bobby said, and hopped onto the back ledge right before the truck left.

"Are you a rider or a driver?" I asked Sam.

"Rider," he said.

I got him up to speed and let go. He coasted for twenty feet.

"Why doesn't everybody ride around on office chairs?" he asked.

"It's a mystery," I said.

17
DRIVING TO THE GROVE

We named our ride Zippy the Chair-i-ot.

My idea.

"Detour to Parrot Kingdom!" Sam shouted.

At PK, Sam stood on Zippy's seat and, for ten minutes, held on to my hair with one hand for balance.

"Come here, birds," he said. "I'll give you food."

Here's what I can tell you: begging parrots is a waste of time.

At the grove, we parked Zippy under the first tree.

"Luckily, the orangest oranges are at the top," Sam said.

I was balancing on a thin branch when an orange whizzed by my head.

"Cut it out, Sam!" I yelled.

"Cut what out?" Sam shouted.

He was behind me, on an even skinnier branch.

Another orange smash-landed on the front of my shirt.

"Hey!" I yelled.

"Hay is for horses," somebody shrieked.

The shrieker was below us. She was wearing a dress with strawberry pockets and a red hair bow. She was sitting on Zippy.

"Ouch!" Sam yelled. "Who threw that?"

"We're under attack!" I shouted.

"I declare War of the Oranges!" a boy yelled.

"Who threw that?" Sam asked again.

"It's Geoffrey," the girl said. "He likes throwing."

"Where is he?" Sam asked.

"Behind the lemon tree," the girl said.

I threw a fastball orange.

"Missed," the girl said.

Geoffrey's next orange hit Sam dead in the head. It cracked open. The orange. Not Sam's head. But it did juice his hair.

"Quit orange-bombing us until we're out of the tree!" I shouted.

"You should've thought of that before you climbed it!" Geoffrey shouted.

"I call time-out," Sam said.

"Time-out doesn't exist!" Geoffrey yelled.

I stepped down a branch and turned around to see Sam. An orange hit the back of my knee. That leg went straight to kneeling position. My other leg slipped. I fell through layers of branches before I landed stomach first on a bottom branch. I folded like a towel.

Sam jumped to the ground.

I dropped two oranges. "Incoming ammunition," I whispered.

Sam bowled one.

The girl intercepted and started peeling.

I did a brave thing.

"You can't hit me!" I shouted.

When he did, Sam did his famous two-handed, two-ball pitch. He double-beaned Geoffrey.

"That's what you get when you pick a fight with a future Boston Red Sox pitcher!" I shouted.

"Truce," Geoffrey yelled.

"No such thing as a truce," Sam said.

Geoffrey walked over and fake smiled. "That was fun, wasn't it?" he asked.

"You attacked with zero warning," Sam said.

"That's how we do orange wars in Miami," Geoffrey said. "Come on. It's just a game."

"Want to take a turn in my spinning chair?" the girl asked me.

"It's our chair," I said.

"Don't you know finders keepers, losers jeepers?" she asked.

"We're the finders," Sam said.

"We brought it here," I said.

"That's where I found it," the girl said.

"When you see a parked car do you say 'I found it' and drive off?" I asked.

"Kids can't drive. Don't you know that?"

"Time to go, Mary Alice," Geoffrey said.

"You're not the boss of me, Geoffrey," she said. Then she whispered to us, "He's a little the boss of me. Because I'm five and he's twelve. Also Aunt Maeve said I have to cooperate with my brother because I'm driving her out of her mind."

"Kids can't drive," I said.

"I already told you that," she said.

Five-year-olds don't get jokes.

"Come on," Geoffrey said.

"Bye, chair boys!"

"My name's Melonhead," I said. "He's Sam."

On the roll home Sam pushed and I carried the orange bag. We stopped at Ernest Hemingway to use the computer to update our friends.

Dear Pip, Jonique, and Lucy Rose,
    Morning news flash! Nana and Jeep
have barking frogs. Also frogs that

leak poison snot. Paradise is paradise.

We have no idea what you are doing
that is EXCELLENT. We're too busy to
guess right now.

Melonhead and Sam

Sam got an email from his mom.

Sweet Sam,

This morning Julia and I got lost
taking Max (Sophia's middle child) to
playcare and Suzanna (the oldest) to
pre-K. Happily, I saw a bakery. The
sweet rolls were almost as good as
Mickey's Stickies from Baking Divas.
When we get home, we'll all go get
treats at Baking Divas, okay?

Hope you're eating right and being
polite.

Love from all of us,
Mom

Dear Mom,

Alligator is the only wrong thing
I've eaten. And my politeness is on
maximum.

Yes to a trip to Baking Divas!
Love,
Sam

I took one last look at the computer.

DB,
    When you get homesick, picture
Daddy and me in your mind. I'm pic-
turing you right now.
                    We love you,
                    Mom

Dear Mom,
    Why would I be homesick? Nana says
Paradise could be our second home.
                    DB

18

IT GETS WORSE

"Did you get lost going to the grove?" Jeep asked.

"Nope," Sam said.

"Did you meet someone nice?" Nana asked.

"Nope," I said.

"Your arms and legs are covered with scratches," Nana said.

"And my face," I told her. "A kid named Geoffrey threw oranges at us."

"You usually enjoy that sort of thing," Jeep said.

"True," I said. "But it was a sneak attack."

"Two against one?" Jeep asked.

"We had double manpower," I said. "But he's twelve."

"Maybe he was trying to make friends," Nana said.

"Flinging fruit at people makes a bad impression," I said.

Since we suffered, Jeep let us work the blender.

Sam handed them their smoothies. "Grandparents first."

"Divine," Nana said.

"Delicious," Jeep said.

"Don't worry about the wall," Sam said. "We'll wash it off."

"It's a long reach," Jeep said.

"Not if we stand on the stove," I said.

"Is that the doorbell?" Sam asked.

"Who can it be?" I said to Nana and Jeep. "You don't have friends."

We all went to the door.

A round lady with carrot-colored hair was standing on the Miami Dolphins doormat, fanning herself with a booklet called "People in Paradise."

"I'm Maeve Mackey," she said. "You're

the only Melons in the phone book. I'm looking for a boy named Melonhead, and another named Sam."

Supersonic brain-to-brain message to Sam: *What did we do?*

When people come to find us, we're usually in trouble.

"I'm Melonhead," I admitted.

Mrs. Mackey yelled over her shoulder, "It's the right house!"

A squeaky voice screamed, "Here I am, chair boys!"

I waved. "Hi, Mary Alice."

Geoffrey walked like he was wading through a pool of used gum.

"My nephew has something to tell you," Mrs. Mackey said.

"Because some things have to be dealt with, didn't you say that, Aunt Maeve?"

"Yes, I did, Mary Alice," Aunt Maeve said.

"You said it when I tattled on Geoffrey. Because

it's lucky those boys didn't fall out of the tree. That's what you said. Then Geoffrey said 'You're a blabbermouth' to me."

Jeep shook Mary Alice's hand.

"Hello, mister," she said. "We don't live here. No kids allowed. My teacher's name is Mr. Lighthouse. I'm not making that up. Aunt Maeve has a cat named Mr. Jingles."

"Mary Alice, you're a good reporter," Nana said.

"I look forward to seeing what she'll do when she's grown," Aunt Maeve said.

"I'm being a car driver and a horse doctor and a cake maker and a teacher who wears fashions," Mary Alice said. "And the boss."

"You will have an interesting life," Jeep said.

"You will too," Mary Alice said.

"Geoffrey," Aunt Maeve said, in the way that means "get on with it."

"I'm sorry for starting a war," he mumbled.

He didn't sound sorry.

Nana gave me a quick XLG.

"Adam, wouldn't you like to accept Geoffrey's apology?" she asked.

"Accepted," I said.

"Ditto," Sam said. "You can't help it if orange wars are different in Miami."

"Geoffrey, don't stand on the porch like a potted plant," Nana said. "Come inside."

"Geoffrey got a math prize because he's in Gifted and Talented," Mary Alice said. "It's a ribbon. That's all. Just a ribbon. A rabbit would be better. That's what I think."

"Congratulations, Geoffrey," Jeep said.

"That's a handsome tie you're wearing, Geoffrey," Nana said. "Are you going somewhere special?"

Geoffrey looked confused. "These are my regular clothes," he said.

"You wear a blazer all the time?" I asked.

"Not in the summer," he said.

"Do kids tease you about it?" I asked.

"Sometimes," he said.

"Can I ride Zippy?" Mary Alice asked.

"Zippy?" Jeep said.

"It's an old office chair with wheels," Geoffrey said.

He made it sound babyish.

"Melonhead gets first turn," Mary Alice said. "Then Sam. Then Geoffrey. That's the order."

"For what?" Geoffrey asked.

"Pushing me around the town," Mary Alice said.

"I admire a girl who can keep order, Mary Alice," Jeep said.

"I'm very great at it," Mary Alice said. "Everybody who's a kid, go outside."

In the back of my ears I heard Nana say, "I'll get us coffee, Maeve. You go into our living room, and when you find the most comfortable chair, sit in it—like Goldilocks."

"You're a kick," Mrs. Mackey said.

That did not sound 3P to me, but Nana acted like it was a compliment.

19

GEOFFREY THE KNOW-IT-ALL

I rolled Zippy and Mary Alice around the block. Twice. Then I passed Zippy to Sam like we were in a relay race.

Geoffrey was in the Melonmobile, trying to look like he was driving.

To give him a chance to be likeable, I sat next to him.

"Mary Alice says I should paint Zippy silver," I told Geoffrey.

"Our mom says she's creative. I don't think putting baby shoes on the dog is creative. It's irritating."

"You have a dog?" I said.

"Two," he said.

"Two dogs?" I said. "For one boy? How did you get them?"

"I asked my dad."

"Just like that he bought you two?"

"I couldn't make up my mind, so he said, 'Get both.'"

Geoffrey wasn't kidding.

"Tom is small and hairy," Geoffrey said. "Pinky is big and hairy. Pinky's a boy but Mary Alice got to name him."

"Can they do tricks?" I asked.

"Pinky dances on his back legs if you hold a treat high enough. Tom can jump through a hula hoop, if it's low."

"Sam's getting a dog," I said, right when Sam and Mary Alice rolled up.

"When are you getting your dog?" Geoffrey asked Sam.

"When I save fifty dollars," Sam said.

"Which means never," Geoffrey said. "I know because I tried it."

"You have enough dogs," I said.

"I tried saving for a bike," he said. "It took too

long. I settled for a pogo stick. I predict you'll settle for a guinea pig."

My mind flashed to when Sam and I were saving up for hockey sticks. On the fourth day, we spent all our money on Starbursts. I think Sam was thinking that too. He had the look of defeat.

"Sam won't be tempted by a cheaper pet," I said. "Because he'll already have a pet. A free pet. We're catching it this week."

Geoffrey smirked. "What can you catch? A turtle?"

Madness crept up my neck and turned it red.

"An alligator," I said. "We're catching a baby alligator."

"An alligator egg," Sam said. "It's going to hatch in our hands."

When Geoffrey laughs, he sounds like a seal.

"Worst idea ever," he said.

Mary Alice poked her brother. "Drive me," she said.

They left. Sam and I sat in the Melonmobile.

"I can't believe I told Geoffrey we're getting a pet alligator," I said.

"I can," Sam said. "You have excellent ideas."

"It's not an idea," I said. "It's a lie. I made it up because Geoffrey was making me furious."

"The alligator can live in our laundry sink," Sam said.

"What about your parents?" I asked.

"They said I can have any pet except a rat, bat, or snake," Sam said. "Nobody said no alligator."

"Getting an alligator egg probably isn't hard," I said. "Turtles swipe them, and they have one-inch arms. Plus they're slow."

"We'd actually be saving the egg from becoming a turtle snack," Sam said. "Like my grandma says, it would be a major mitzvah."

"A good deed?" I said. "It would be a magnificent deed."

Geoffrey pushed Zippy up the driveway and sent Mary Alice inside.

"What do alligator nests look like?" Sam asked.

"A mound of mud covered with vegetation,"

Geoffrey said. "The egg season starts in July and ends in the fall."

"Excellent," I said. "We're on time."

"You have to stay twenty feet away, at least," Geoffrey said. "My encyclopedia of reptiles says mother alligators are protective."

"So is Melonhead's," Sam said.

Geoffrey sat sideways on the Melonmobile's backseat.

"His mom doesn't bite or grow nine feet long," Geoffrey said.

"We're not going to reach in, grab an egg, and run," I said. "We're not foolish."

"We'll wait until the mom goes swimming," Sam said. "Then we'll scoop up an egg with Nana's crab net."

"One egg," I said. "She has a whole clutch. She won't notice."

"She'll notice," Geoffrey said.

"Can you tell if it's a girl egg or a boy egg?" Sam asked.

"In a nest, every egg's the same. All girls or all boys," he said.

"Seriously?" I said.

"I'm always serious," Geoffrey said. "If the temperature in the nest is over ninety degrees, they'll all be boys. If it's under eighty-six, they'll all be girls. You should know more before you go egg hunting."

"We know what we're doing," I said.

"No, you don't," Geoffrey said.

Like my dad says, some people love to argue.

"We just have to get the mom interested in something else," Sam said.

"Nothing can distract a mother gator," Geoffrey said.

"An Alligator Distractor can," I said. Geoffrey's know-it-all attitude made me blurt it before I thought.

"There's no such thing," Geoffrey said.

"There will be," Sam said. "We're inventors."

"Are you working in the Jimmy Buffet Woodworking Room?" Geoffrey asked.

"Is it in the clubhouse?" Sam asked.

Geoffrey nodded. "I could help you invent," he said. "My teacher says I've got untapped abilities."

"The Distractor's a two-man job," I said.

"Thanks anyway," Sam said.

20

HORSING AROUND

Aunt Maeve sent Geoffrey out back to get Mary Alice.
Nana gave Sam and me a look that meant "go with
him."

Mary Alice and Jeep were by the canal. Jeep
looked like a pioneer lady, if a pioneer lady had an
apron tied around her head instead of a hat and was
crawling on her hands and knees with yellow rubber gloves stretched over her feet. From the back Jeep
looked like he had giant chicken feet that had been
put on backward.

"Be a good show pony!" Mary Alice shouted.

Jeep neighed.

Mary Alice fake-snapped her fingers and screamed, "Jump, Pauline!"

"Your name is Pauline?" I asked Jeep.

"Don't I look like a Pauline?" he said.

"Prance, Pauline," Mary Alice demanded. "Prance on your pony legs."

Jeep was still wearing his apron hat and chicken feet when we were saying good-bye in the front yard.

"Maeve," Nana said. "Thanks for offering to keep an eye on the boys when we're at work."

"Geoffrey and Mary Alice are welcome anytime," Jeep said.

Mary Alice walked backwards across the grass, yelling, "I miss you, Pauline. You were the best horse I ever had."

"Nana," I said. "You should ask Ms. Mackey to be your friend. She's nice so she probably won't mind."

"Do you like Geoffrey more than you did?" Jeep asked.

"Better than when he was clobbering us," Sam said.

"Not much better," I said. "He's bossy."

"Geoffrey might be a little buttoned-up for you," Jeep said.

I thought he was talking about Geoffrey's shirt. It turned out buttoned-up is a type of personality.

When we went back inside, Nana said I should email my mom and dad. Sam too. He went first.

Dear Mom,
     Melonhead and I are having fun. Most of it's not when we're with a kid named Geoffrey. He is here visiting his aunt.
     I'm bringing home a grand surprise for the family.
                         Love,
                         Sam

P.S. It's eleven o'clock a.m. here.
What time is it in Philadelphia?

Dear Sam,
    I'm delighted you are bringing
home a surprise for our family. Your
thoughtfulness makes me proud.
    Julia and I are excited to see
what it is!
    It's the same time in Florida as
it is in Philadelphia. It's Dad who
is in another time zone.
    I miss you, honey.
                         Love,
                         Mom

Then it was my turn.

Dear Dad,
    We are busy and doing good stuff.
Sam and I are inventing an Alligator
Distractor.
                    Love,
                    Melonhead

We got some juice from the kitchen. I found an
answer when we came back.

Dear Sport,

   Glad you are keeping out of trouble. Where are these alligators you
hope to distract?

                         Love,
                         Dad

21

BACK TO THE PONCE

"Let's go!" Jeep hollered. "Bridge on the Johnny Depp Terrace."

"We're coming!" I shouted from the pantry.

"I hope the bridge is suspended," Sam said.

"And sways when you walk on it," I said. "And goes over a ravine filled with piranhas."

"Boys?" Jeep yelled.

"One minute, please!" I yelled. "We're loading up on marshmallows."

"Stuff your pockets," Sam said. "Smash the air out. Velcro them shut before they reinflate."

"Good thing the military invented cargo shorts,"

I said. "And good thing we ate all my emergency cereal."

I never leave without four pockets full, but Nana and Jeep only eat bran. I'm anti-bran.

We licked stick dirt off our hands.

"Job one: invent the Distractor," Sam said. "Job two: find alligator nest."

"We'll see some nests at the beach, I think. But to be safe, you should pick a backup pet."

"Pig's my backup," Sam said. "Backup to my backup is a parrot."

"All aboard the Melonmobile," Nana said.

Since we ride backwards, Sam and I flipped our baseball caps and sunned our tantoos. "Where are the wild pigs in Paradise?" I shouted.

"No gators. No pigs," Jeep said.

"How can they call it Paradise?" I screamed.

"We might catch a pet pig for me," Sam said.

My grandparents laughed.

"I want a pig like the one on the commercial!" Sam hollered. "A tiny runt, the color of my sister's room. With personality."

"Only it'll be muddy because of being wild," I said.

"You're taking your pig on the plane?" Jeep asked.

"If it fits under the seat," Sam said.

"If it doesn't, you and Nana can drive it up when you come for Thanksgiving. E-Z P-Z lickety-split."

"Running a pig carpool tops our bucket list," Jeep said.

"It'll be fun on wheels," I said. "A pig in the car is built-in entertainment."

From the way Jeep was laughing you'd have thought he had an entertaining pig in the Melon-mobile.

"Wild pigs aren't pink or cute," Nana said. "They're disgusting."

"One person's disgusting is another person's cute," I said. "Pigs are our cute."

"Wild pigs are hairy," Jeep said. "They squeal like sirens. The boars have razor-sharp tusks."

"That's exciting," I said.

"Boars are wild pigs," Nana repeated, and added, "They're fearless and not at all nice."

"I thought they'd be like Wilbur in *Charlotte's*

Web," Sam said. "Without the talking. That's fiction."

"Have you city boys seen a live pig?" Jeep asked.

"This will be our first," I said.

"They can get as big as refrigerators," Jeep said.

"I'm shocked," Sam said.

22

DISAPPOINTING NEWS

"First came the orange war," I said. "Then the pig news. Now there's no bridge on the terrace. Just people playing cards."

"It's been a tough morning," Nana said.

"You'll have fun working on your invention," Jeep said. "Meet us in the Welcome Room at twelve-thirty."

The WR has glass walls and makes you feel like you're in a space station. The information table is glass with curved edges, like an upside-down *U*. I bet it was invented by NASA. You can't have corners in zero gravity.

"You don't need to ring the bell for service when I'm sitting here," the Information Lady said.

"We don't mind," I told her.

Her badge said LOVEY.

"If my name was Lovey, I'd change it the second I heard it," I whispered to Sam.

Who knew she has supersonic hearing? Not me.

"I like my name," Lovey said.

"Ditto," I said. "I mean, I don't like *your* name. I like *my* name. Melonhead. But my mom doesn't."

"Do you have any questions about Paradise or St. Augustine?" she asked.

"Where are the alligators?" Sam asked.

"Paradise is an alligator-free zone," Lovey said.

"We know," I said. "What we want is a free alligator zone."

"Sorry to disappoint," she said.

"It's not your fault," Sam told her. "I blame the underwater fence."

"Is that bowl of M&M'S for the Convenience of the Residents?" I asked.

"Help yourself," she said.

We did. "Four hands, four handfuls," I said.

I poured one handful in my mouth and dumped the other in a pocket to mix with the marshmallows.

"On to the Jimmy Buffet Woodworking Room!" Sam yelled.

"Better hurry," Lovey said.

23

THE JIMMY BUFFET ROOM

Sam karate-kicked open the door.

He jumped back.

"People are in the Jimmy Buffet," he whispered.

"Come in," said a lady with curly silver hair.

"Thanks," I said.

"Who do you belong to?" she asked.

"My parents," I said.

"Ditto," Sam said. "Only mine are different parents."

"Whom are you visiting in Paradise?" she asked.

"The Melons," Sam said.

"I don't know them," the lady said.

"You should," I said. "They need friends."

"They are Melonhead's grandparents," Sam said.

"I'm Tom Thompson," a man said.

He was as bald as an upside-down cereal bowl.

A short guy shook my hand.

"I'm Squinty," he said.

"I know why," I said. "When you smile, your eyes look like dashes."

He smiled and they did.

"This is our friend Mrs. Fontaine," Squinty said.

"Care to make a birdhouse?" Mr. Thompson asked.

"We won't know what kind of house we need until we have a pet to put in it," Sam said.

"We're here to invent an Alligator Distractor," I explained.

"Mr. Thompson can help," Mrs. Fontaine said. "He's a rocket scientist."

"Are you kidding?" Sam asked.

Squinty laughed. "I hope not. He worked at the Kennedy Space Station in Cape Canaveral for thirty years. Got paid for it."

"How much?" I asked.

"Not saying," Mr. Thompson said.

"I have curiosity about money," I said.

"It's one of our biggest interests," Sam said.

"An Alligator Distractor is a marvelous idea," Mrs. Fontaine said. "If an alligator was nipping at my ankles, I'd be quite desperate to distract it."

"I guess it could work for that too," I said.

"How does one distract an alligator?" Mr. Thompson asked.

"Marshmallows," I said. "We learned that from the TV show we watched on the airplane."

"Any alligator with a brain the size of a walnut, which, in fact, is the size of every alligator brain, would literally leap at the opportunity to eat a marshmallow," Mr. Thompson said.

"Florida's crawling with alligators," Squinty said.

"Exactly where are these alligators?" I asked.

I wished someone would answer that question.

"How does the Distractor work?" Squinty asked.

"Like an electric slingshot," I said.

"Press a button. A marshmallow flies out," Sam said. "The alligator chases it."

"The only rough spot I see is that it's illegal to feed wild alligators," Mr. Thompson said.

"How are they supposed to get food?" I asked.

"They find plenty of food," Squinty said. "But when people feed them, alligators start thinking of humans as food suppliers."

"That would be good," I said. "They'd be our friends."

"They're not a grateful species," Mr. Thompson said.

"What if marshmallows were the only way to save yourself?" I asked.

"You'd be alive but arrested," Sam said.

"I think the police would forgive a life- or limb-saving marshmallow," Squinty said.

"Alligators rarely attack," Mrs. Fontaine said. "They don't like people."

"Our taste or our personalities?" I asked.

They laughed. I pretended I was trying to be hilarious.

"Some are curious," Squinty said. "Remember that seven-foot gator that followed kids to Forest Lakes Elementary?"

"What happened?" I asked.

"The crossing guard called the sheriff," he said. "A deputy came. The first thing he did was climb on top of a wall."

Mrs. Fontaine interrupted. "Before the deputy could lasso it, the gator thrashed and broke off a hunk with its tail."

"A hunk of deputy?" Sam asked.

"A hunk of wall," she said. "The deputy was a trained alligator wrangler."

"Are wranglers like cowboys for reptiles?" Sam asked.

Mrs. Fontaine nodded. "He wrangled it, roped it, and taped its mouth shut."

"How long was school canceled?" Sam asked.

"In Florida, school does not stop for a nuisance alligator," Squinty said.

"Who calls a seven-foot alligator a nuisance?" I asked.

"Floridians," Mr. Thompson said.

24
MAKING PLANS

Mrs. Fontaine found paper so we could draw our design. Squinty gave us the golf pencil he keeps behind his ear. I'm going to start that habit. Sam too. Only we're doing it behind both of our ears.

I drew a long tube.

"Do you blow it like a spitball?" Mrs. Fontaine asked.

"You'd need an elephant's worth of breath," I said.

"Add the button," Sam said. "And a handle."

"Let's see if your design's any good," Mr. Thompson said.

"We need pipes," Sam said.

"Mr. Clarke, the maintenance man, brought a cart full of plastic pipes to my apartment when he fixed my air conditioner," Mrs. Fontaine said. "I'll see if he'll bring it over."

When I saw that box, I said, "I feel like we won a contest."

"Use what you need," Mr. Clarke said. "Here's a box of extras. And I figure you'll want plumbing tape and a ball valve."

"What's that?" Sam asked.

"It's like an on and off switch," he said.

"We need it," I said.

"Can you spare primer cement?" Squinty asked.

"Sure," Mr. Clarke said.

"If we had a balloon, we could blow it up in the tube," I said. "When we popped it the air would whoosh through the pipe and push the marshmallow out."

"Good hypothesis," Mr. Thompson said.

"If you pop from the back the air will whoosh out the back," Sam said.

"If you pop it from the front, the marshmallow will whoosh out in your face," I said.

I ate a marshmallow while I thought.

"Remember the cereal incident?" I asked.

"When we put the hose on the wrong end of the vacuum," Sam said. "It sprayed dirt all over the kitchen."

"What if we hook it up wrong on purpose?" I said. "Drop a marshmallow in the metal tube. Press ON and *zing!* That baby's flying."

"That could work," Mr. Thompson said.

"E-Z P-Z. Just bring your vacuum wherever you go," Sam said.

"There are no electrical outlets in drainage ditches," Squinty said. "But sometimes there are alligators."

I ate six more marshmallows. Then I shouted, "Brainflash of Brilliance! We need a drill."

"In the cabinet," Mrs. Fontaine said.

"I wish we were over sixty," Sam said. "I love living in Paradise."

"Do we have zip ties?" I asked.

"Right here," Mr. Thompson said.

Squinty and I measured and marked. Sam painted purple glue  on pipes.

Mr. Thompson and I hack-  sawed.

"I'll drill," Sam said. "Can somebody find a plastic cap in the extras box? That could keep air from escaping."

"I'll drill," Mrs. Fontaine said. "You look for the cap."

Sorry to say it, but she is a tool hog.

"Zip-tie the pipes together," Sam said.

We got a ton done by twelve-thirty.

"We've got a golf game to get to," Squinty said then.

"We have grandparents waiting," I told him. "But we'll be back to- morrow."

"We're going to see the cut-glass display at the Lightener Museum," Mrs. Fontaine said.

"I'm dead sorry," I said. "We can't come with you."

"Due to being busy," Sam said.

"But thanks for inviting us," I said.

"Can you finish the Distractor the day after tomorrow?" Mrs. Fontaine asked. "I'd like to see it in action."

"Sure, they can," a squeaky voice said.

Mary Alice marched into the room. Geoffrey followed.

"Hi, chair boys! It's me, Mary Alice. Do you remember me? I came to your house."

"Of course we remember you," I said. "We saw you three hours ago."

"I remember you too," she said. "Probably so does Geoffrey, because he's smarter than everybody. That's what you said, right, Geoffrey?"

"That's *not* what I said, Mary Alice."

Geoffrey's ears were as purple as Jeep's sofa.

"Is that the Alligator Distractor?" he asked.

"All that's left to do is figure out how to get it to launch a marshmallow," Mrs. Fontaine said.

"I have an idea," Geoffrey said.

"We're loaded with ideas," I said.

"I didn't think you could make it work," Geoffrey said.

"I do think it," Mary Alice said.

25

THEY WON'T STOP FOLLOWING US

Nana and Jeep were in the Welcome Room.

"What's next?" I asked.

"Fencing class," Jeep said.

"Hot diggity dog in a fog," I said. "I've been begging my mom to sign me up for sword fighting at Parks and Rec."

"I'm afraid Paradise management won't let children jab each other with swords," Jeep said. "Very untrusting of them."

"I could jab you," I said. "Sam can jab Nana."

"How about yoga?" Nana asked.

"I'd rather wear shorts made of bees," I said.

"Doll," Jeep said. "What's the worst that can happen if we leave the boys here?"

"Don't think of the worst," I said.

"They'd be by themselves for three hours," she said.

"This will be a trial run. They'll be on their own when we're at work," Jeep said.

"How would you feel if you were left alone?" Nana asked us.

"Free," I said. "And excited."

They laughed.

"So we'll try this. We'll count on you. Eat these sandwiches I made for Jeep," Nana said. "We'll get protein bars at the fitness center."

"We'll meet you out front at three-ten," Jeep said.

"Have a good sword fight," Sam said.

"I always win," Nana whispered.

They took off in the Melonmobile.

Sam and I sat on the golden turtles in Ponce's fountain and ate Jeep's marmalade sandwiches.

"This is the life," I said.

"Being old is a sweet deal," Sam said.

"They're following us," I whispered.

"Old people?" Sam asked.

"Hey," Geoffrey said.

"Hi," I said.

I gave Sam a look so he'd know what I was thinking.

Mary Alice climbed into the fountain without taking off her sandals.

"Do not say 'Get out' to me, Geoffrey," Mary Alice said.

Geoffrey didn't. He just sat on the edge, dangling his feet.

"Have you given up on getting an alligator egg yet?" he asked.

"Nope," Sam said.

"What will you do when it hatches?" Geoffrey asked.

"Name it," I said.

"Tame it," Sam said.

"Alligators don't tame," Geoffrey said. "It'll get too big for your house."

"Dr. Garcia, who is an actual

expert, said when they're young, they grow a foot a year," I replied. "Not an actual foot. A twelve-inch foot."

"In two years we'll have earned fifty bucks," Sam said.

"Then we'll give our two-foot alligator to the National Zoo," I said. "We'll take the dog to visit it on weekends."

"Young alligators can climb fences," Geoffrey said.

"With those short legs?" Sam asked. "I doubt it."

"Adult gators can jump six feet high," Geoffrey said.

"Like velociraptors?" I asked.

"Yep," Geoffrey said.

"Cool," Sam said.

"I'd say if a six-year-old can hatch an alligator in his hands, it'll be a snap for two eleven-year-olds," I said.

"Tell the alligators, 'Don't bite people. I mean it.' That's all," Mary Alice said.

"Dogs bite more people than alligators do," Geoffrey said.

"So you're saying it's safer to get an alligator than a dog," I said.

"That's not what I meant," Geoffrey said.

I felt good for defending alligators and bad for criticizing dogs.

"A baby gator bite probably feels like a human baby bite," Sam said. "Neither of them have teeth."

"First of all, baby alligators are called grunts," Geoffrey said. "Grunts grow up. They get seventy-four to eighty-eight super-sharp teeth. When one falls out, another grows in."

"Really?" I asked.

"Some alligators go through three thousand teeth in their lives," Geoffrey said.

"Like pencils that automatically get resharpened," I said. "That's tremendous."

"I read it in *Alligator Facts Every Floridian Should Know,*" Geoffrey said. "Most people who read it are in high school."

"What if every Floridian doesn't want to know alligator facts?" Sam asked.

"They do," Geoffrey said. "The alligator is the Official Florida State Animal. And we have a football team called the Florida Gators."

"That alligator that followed kids to school didn't nip a single one," Sam said.

"They don't bite a lot of people," Geoffrey said. "Only one in two point six million."

"Which is nothing," I said.

"Unless you're the one," Geoffrey said.

26

THE DAVE BARRY BUFFET

"Sixty-six minutes are done," Mary Alice said. "The fountain is over."

"Try six minutes," Geoffrey said.

"Time for cheese sandwiches," Mary Alice said.

"You can't get food at the Ponce," Sam said.

"Sure you can," Mary Alice said. "Otherwise, you'd be hungry."

"You don't know about the Dave Barry Buffet?" Geoffrey asked.

"Doesn't matter," I said. "We don't have any money."

"If we did, we'd save it for a dog," Sam said.

"It doesn't cost money," Mary Alice said.

"It's for the Convenience of the Residents?" I asked. "Like tennis and oranges?"

"Yep," Geoffrey said. "You just sign your name."

"It's called autograph," Mary Alice said. "You can do it if you know letters."

"Hot diggity dog on a hog," I said.

Mary Alice's dress dripped fountain water up the ramp, down the hall, and into the restaurant.

"Wave at Ms. Fadul," Mary Alice said. "I'm not allowed to call her Nora because I am a child. When I'm sixty or forty-eleven I can say Nora. Right, Ms. Fadul?"

Ms. Fadul smiled. "Hello, Mary Alice," she said.

"For your surprise I brought boys named Sam and Melonhead," Mary Alice told her.

Ms. Fadul smiled at us. "What are your grandparents' names?" she asked.

"The Melons," I said.

"They do not have a head," Mary Alice said. "Just Melonhead does. That's all."

"His grandparents have heads," Geoffrey said.

"Do they know you're here?" Ms. Fadul asked.

"They're the ones who brought us," I said.

"Enjoy lunch," Ms. Fadul said.

Sam and I got thirteen foods to split, counting two Oranginas.

"I wish we knew about this yesterday," I said. "I feel sad about all the food we missed."

"I wish we had a free restaurant at home," Sam said.

"Ditto," I said.

"Ditto," Geoffrey said.

Copycat, I thought.

27
ALL I CAN EAT

We sat in a booth.

"What happens when you don't get an alligator egg?" Geoffrey asked.

"If I don't get an egg, I'll get a parrot," Sam said.

Geoffrey laughed. "They're uncatchable."

"Get a worm," Mary Alice said. "Worms are smart, I think. They eat dirt, right? And probably water. Everybody drinks water. Even fish. Right, Geoffrey?"

"Right, Mary Alice," Geoffrey said.

"We have worms at home," I said.

"Do you like snakes?" Mary Alice asked.

"Who doesn't?" I said.

"Change your mind," she said. "The corral snake can kill you dead with poison."

"It's a coral snake, Mary Alice," Geoffrey said. "Coral is a dark orange color. A corral is a place for horses."

"And it's yellow and black," she said. "It's made of stripes."

Geoffrey rolled his eyes. "She just learned the rhyme," he said.

"What rhyme?" Sam asked.

"The one everybody in Florida learns at school," Geoffrey said. "The rhyme about how to tell the difference between a killer coral snake and a harmless scarlet snake."

"Red touches yellow, kills a fellow. Red touches black, friend of Jack!" Mary Alice yelled.

"I never heard of that in my entire life," I said.

"I never heard of a coral snake," Sam said.

"So if you see one, remember the stripe pattern is the key," Geoffrey added. "Red, black, yellow is good. Red, yellow, black is poison."

"I want a Florida pet," Sam said.

"Like Big Girl," Mary Alice said. "She lives in our

backyard. I'm not allowed to bring her inside anymore. That's a rule."

"Big Girl's an iguana," Geoffrey said. "She might be a boy. Mary Alice named her."

"Iguanas are almost as good as dinosaurs," Sam said.

"Big Girl sleeps in a tree. She's going to grow a mile. Right, Geoffrey?"

"Maybe seven feet," Geoffrey said.

"Seven feet or a mile," Mary Alice said. "She has giant toenails."

"How come nobody told us Florida has iguanas?" Sam asked.

"It didn't used to," Geoffrey said. "People bought them at pet stores, got bored, and let them go. After a while there were so many free iguanas that they met each other and had families."

"Who could get bored with an iguana?" Sam said.

"Who'd give up an animal that has built-in armor and back spikes?" I said.

"Who'd give up an animal with a dewlap?" Geoffrey said.

"What's a dewlap?" I asked.

"The baggy skin that hangs under their chins," Geoffrey said.

Supersonic b-to-b message to Sam: *I admit it: Geoffrey knows a load about animals.*

"Where are the iguana trees?" Sam asked.

"Oh, there are no iguanas in St. Augustine," Geoffrey said. "It's too cold."

"Geoffrey," I said. "Is there any animal in Paradise that isn't rare, doesn't have replaceable teeth or razor-sharp tusks, doesn't get as big as a refrigerator, and is likeable?"

"Sure there is," Mary Alice said. "It's called alarmadillo!"

"Armadillo," Geoffrey told her.

"That's not the same thing I'm talking about," Mary Alice said.

"We've never seen an armadillo," Sam said.

"Alarmadillos sparkle," Mary Alice said. "They eat cake and raisins. You have to sing 'Weensy Spider' to them or they can't sleep."

Geoffrey rolled his eyes. "They have armor and

pointy heads. One armadillo can suck up forty thousand ants for breakfast."

"Cancel the armadillo," I said.

"Don't cancel alarmadillos!" Mary Alice squeaked.

"Sorry," Sam said. "But we can't find forty thousand ants."

"Get forty thousand raisins," Mary Alice said. "They don't know the difference."

"Armadillos eat all insects," Geoffrey said. "My uncle says if you have enough bugs in your yard, armadillos will find you."

"Even my mom would go for a bug-eating pet," I said. "What else do you know about armadillos?"

Geoffrey shrugged. "I only read about sharks, skinks, and alligators."

"Lovey will know if armadillos live in Paradise," Sam said.

"That's using your noodle, Poodle," I said.

Noodle is Pop's word for brain.

"I want a rhyme," Mary Alice said.

"You live in a palace, Mary Alice," I said.

"With show ponies," she said. "And dewlaps. And Geoffrey."

"You can't live with dewlaps, Mary Alice," Geoffrey said.

"I can if I want," she said.

"Let's stop off at the Ernest Hemingway Lounge," I said. "It's time for an email check."

I had one from my mom.

> DB,
>   Are you using sunblock?
>   Remember to be polite. Remind Sam, too.
>   Compliment your grandparents.
>   Your aunts and cousins send their love.
>   Love,
>   Mom

> Dear Mom,
>   1. Yes to sunblock.
>   2. I'm remembering. Sam is too.
>   3. I'm ahead on compliments. I told Nana that she has a cool dewlap.
>   Love,
>   DB

> P.S. Would you like a pet that eats bugs?

28

LOVEY

After we finished lounging, we stopped off at the Welcome Center to see if Lovey had reloaded the M&M'S bowl yet and to ask about armadillos.

A man was talking to her about golfing.

"Excuse me," I said. Twice, to be polite.

Lovey didn't notice us until I was pouring the bowl of fresh M&M'S into Sam's pocket.

"Hello, boys. Who are your friends?" she asked.

"He's Geoffrey," I said. "The girl under the table is Mary Alice."

Mary Alice was pushing her nostrils up against the glass. "I'm an alarmadillo!" she yelled. "I eat ants with my nose."

"Let me help you get out, dear," Lovey said, not in a soft way.

Mary Alice dragged her smushed nose to the edge of the underneath side of the glass table and knee-walked out.

"Are armadillos loyal?" Sam asked Lovey.

Lovey was looking at the line of snot smeared across the bottom of the top of her glass desk.

"Hold down the fort, Joe," she said to the golfing guy. "I'll get the Windex."

"Armadillos are as loyal as they are beautiful," Joe said.

"Smart?" Sam asked.

"Some are smarter than others," Joe said.

"Do armadillos live in Paradise?" I asked.

"Many do," he said.

"Baby alarmadillos are small as toenails," Mary Alice said.

"They're the size of a golf ball," Joe said. "And they're always identical quintuplets."

"Armadillo jackpot!" I said.

"Where do they hang out?" Sam asked.

"Wherever they want," Joe said. "You don't see them because they're nocturnal."

"I'm back," Lovey said. "What was your question?"

"Joe answered it," Sam said. "Thanks."

We went outside.

"An armadillo is no dog," I said. "But it's a pet you can be proud of."

"It's my fourth choice," Sam said. "After alligator and parrot. Dog is always number one."

"Here comes Pauline!" Mary Alice screamed.

I socked Sam's arm.

"Quick, Nick. Turn your hat around."

"Does my tantoo show?"

"More than it did, kid," I said. "How's mine?"

"Nice," he said.

The Melonmobile stopped by the curb. "Hop on, boys," Jeep said. "We're going on a surprise outing. Nana's idea."

Supersonic b-to-b message to Sam: *Warning! Grand-mother ideas are usually dull.*

"Nana," Sam said, "please tell me we're not going clothes shopping."

She smiled in a way that gave me no hope at all.

When she told us I screamed, "May I use your phone, Nana?"

```
LR, J & P, Zip lining over pits of
alligators! No joke. More news soon.
M & S

M & S, Yr grandparents let you hang
over gator pits? We don't believe it.
LR, J & P

LR, J & P, Believe it. It's true!
M & S
```

I emailed my dad about our adventure later.

```
Dear Dad,
    Jeep and Nana let us ride the zip
line at the alligator farm! It was
your mother's idea. They waited for
us at the end and bought us T-shirts
that say I SURVIVED ALLIGATOR CROSSING.
They're rare. You can only buy them
if you survive.
    At feeding time, we saw an alliga-
```

tor swallow a whole chicken. It didn't even chew. The alligator, I mean. The chicken couldn't. It was frozen.

Sam doesn't want a pet alligator anymore. I agree with him.

Love,
Melonhead

P.S. Is the Congressman still a loser?

P.P.S. Is the zip line another thing I shouldn't tell Mom until we're back home?

He wrote back.

Sport and Sam,

The zip line took courage.

I'm proud of you.

I'm glad Sam no longer wants a pet gator. That was never going to happen.

And yes. Hold on to the zip line report until you can tell Mom in person.

Dad

29

THE GREAT BUG HUNT

I called my dad at six a.m. Once he was awake, I said, "Sam and I are collecting bugs in case we need them."

"I was a bug collector when I was ten. I started with houseflies and worked up to centipedes," he said. "Nana's only rule was what lives outside stays outside."

"She still has that rule," I said.

When I got outside, Sam already had a spider.

"I brought Nana's to-go coffee mug," I said. "It's got a built-in air hole in the top."

We flipped our hats and got to work.

An hour later, Sam counted.

"Only thirty-nine thousand, nine hundred ninety-four bugs to go," he said.

"Even an infant armadillo would starve," I said.

"Free the prisoners," Sam said.

I picked them out of their bug villa.

"The spider is down to two legs," I said. "Also, dead."

We rubbed dirt on our tantoos. So it wouldn't be obvious, we also smeared some on our arms and stomachs.

I put Nana's mug by the dish drainer and got nine mini-cheeses.

"Before-breakfast snack attack," I said.

"I told my mom I was bringing home a surprise," Sam said. "She's going to be so disappointed."

"I'll ask Jeep what to do," I said.

We had to bang on the bathroom door until he answered. Half his face was covered with shaving cream.

"Our bug hunt was a flop," I said.

"Did you look in the grove?" he asked. "Bugs are mad for fruit."

"You're a genius!" I said.

"The Melons have good minds," Jeep said. "And you have one of our best."

We stuck around to watch him shave.

30

COFFEE WITH MILK AND LEGS

If our minds weren't on armadillos, one of us would have noticed that Nana was drinking coffee from the bug villa. If I had, I would have stopped her from swallowing the spider legs. When I did notice, it was too late.

"Your Red Cross clothes make you look official," Sam told Nana and Jeep.

Nana smiled. "We are official."

"Want to come to work with us?" Jeep asked. "We'll be up the street at the Janet Reno Exercise Center."

"We're trying to get our neighbors to give up some blood," Nana said.

"That could be why you are having a friends shortage," I said. "No offense."

"Can we watch blood spurt out of customers?" Sam asked.

"No," Jeep said.

"Then no thanks," I said. "We're going bug hunting at the grove."

"Call when you get there," Nana said.

"If you get home first, the key's under the fish mat," Jeep said. "Emergency phone numbers are on the fridge."

Nana put Mrs. Mackey's number in Jeep's phone and gave it back to me. "Call me when you get where you're going and Maeve if you need anything."

"The boys have common sense," Jeep said. "They'll be fine."

31
THE GREAT BUG HUNT, PART TWO

I called Nana from Parrot Kingdom.

Sam called her when we were leaving Parrot Kingdom.

I called my dad on the way to the grove and left a message. Then I called Nana to tell her we were there.

"Stop. Drop. Flop!" I shouted. "This is a gold mine of bugs."

"A bug mine," Sam said.

"Every rotten orange is a bug hotel," I said.

"Beetles!" Sam screamed.

"I have forty thousand ants already!" I yelled.

I pulled my shirtfront into a hammock and put the bug oranges in gently.

"Come look at my gnat collection," Sam said.

"Bring it over, Rover."

Sam took one step. "The gnats flew away," he yelled. "Why are you hopping around like you're on an invisible pogo stick?"

"Ants are running all over my stomach!" I shouted. "And my back!"

"Shake them off," Sam said.

"They're in my armpits!" I shouted.

"Take off your shirt!" Sam hollered.

He pulled his off and slapped it against my back.

"They're falling off," he said.

"They're falling *in*!" I shouted.

"What?" Sam asked.

"I have ants in my pants," I said.

Sam laughed so hard he burped.

"Pants or underpants?" he screamed.

"Both," I said. "Be my lookout. I'm going behind

that lime tree to take off my shorts. It's the only way to de-ant them."

"The coast is clear!" Sam shouted.

I was jumping around in my underpants, shaking my cargo shorts, when I heard something.

"Do you see anybody?" I shouted to Sam.

"Only you," someone said.

I flipped around.

An old lady was standing there.

"Are you OK?" she asked.

I grabbed my shorts and ran like hurricane wind.

"Get on Zippy!" Sam yelled. "I'll push."

If this ever happens to you, do not try to put on your shorts while kneeling on a moving getaway chair.

Sam would not stop singing.

"The ants go marching down your pants,
Hurrah, hurrah.
The little one stops to do a dance,
Hurrah, Hurrah!"

"Ants in My Pants is going on my List of Achievements," I said.

Being in the rider's seat gives you time to think about your life. I started off with hard things, like catching a parrot and collecting forty thousand bugs. I moved to easy things like catching an armadillo once you have bugs.

"Make a U-turn!" I yelled.

I called Nana and said we were back at the grove. Actually, Sam was at the grove. He said the lady wouldn't recognize me with my clothes on but I hid across the street.

Sam made his T-shirt into a bag. I steered Zippy. Due to the neck hole in the bottom of the orange bag, we had to stop a lot to round up the roll-aways.

I dialed Nana. "We're home. Are you getting much blood?"

"Donors are lined up," she said. "We'll be another hour, at least."

Sam squished bananas. I cut up the skins with Nana's sewing scissors.

"Add kiwi, blueberries, and all the sugar in this bowl," I

said. "I'll get a bucket from the garage and meet you outside."

We squeezed the fruit into mush. The oranges were E-Z P-Z. Most of them got presmashed on the way home.

"Taste this, Chris," Sam said.

"Sweet, Pete."

We stashed the bucket of Armadillo Attractor under a yucca plant on the side of the house.

32

THE SHOCK OF OUR LIVES

Sam and I sat on the deck, improving our tantoos, fooling with Jeep's binoculars, and enjoying Oreos.

We're team eaters. I scrape off the insides with my teeth. Sam eats the chocolate cookie outsides.

"I feel like we're at a motel," Sam said. "Except without a pool and with a canal."

"Look! Dragonflies playing air tag," I said.

"Where?"

"Over the water."

"Hand me the binoculars," he said.

Suddenly, it was like a tornado sucked the oxygen out of my lungs. I was airless. I couldn't breathe. Luckily, I could scream.

"Al-li-ga-tor!" I yelled. "Canal! I see eyes. Tail! Twelve feet long."

Sam bolted up.

"Where?"

"Right there. Floating!"

Sam ran smack into the screen door. His face made a dent.

"The handle's stuck!" he yelled.

"Pull!" I shouted.

"Is the gator in the yard?" Sam yipped.

I looked. "No, but it could do a velociraptor jump any second."

"Door's open!" Sam shouted.

I shoved him through and followed.

We collapsed on the tile floor.

"Oh, my sweet feet, we could have been eaten," I said.

"I'm shaking," Sam said.

"Ditto," I said. "Who do we call?"

"Nana and Jeep," Sam said.

"They're too old to wrangle an alligator," I said.

Sam got the emergency phone list. I called Wildlife Control.

"Calm down," the operator said. "What's the address?"

I read it off an envelope from Florida Power and Light.

"I'm dispatching a team to Faye Dunaway Drive," she said. "Stay inside."

"Guard the front!" I yelled to Sam. "I'll tip over the table and push it against the kitchen door for protection."

"Nana and Jeep are home!" Sam shouted.

"Tell them to run!" I yelled.

Sam opened the front door a crack. "Go away!" he yelled.

"What's happening in there?" Jeep shouted.

"Wildlife Control just arrived!" Nana shouted.

"It's about time," I said.

Sam flung open the door.

My grandparents were standing behind two officers.

"Where are the other wranglers?" I said.

"Two is standard," the lady officer said. "But we're two of the best. I'm Asha Mathur. This is Kai Polozie. Did you phone in an alligator sighting?"

I nodded like a bobblehead.

"Officers," Jeep said. "I'm sorry. This is a false alarm. There are no alligators in Paradise."

"Wrong!" I said. "One's in the canal."

"It's twelve feet long," Sam said. "At least."

"We'll check it out," Officer Polozie said. "Stay inside."

"Officer Mathur has an alligator tattoo on her arm," Sam said. "You probably get that for being an expert."

That made me feel a little better.

Jeep wanted to stand on the deck. Nana said he had to set a good example. He said it was safe to untip the table. I didn't agree.

We watched through the screen door.

"I hope Officer Polozie doesn't fall in the canal," Nana said.

My stomach shrank into a marble.

"Don't provoke the alligator," I yelled. "Think of your arm!"

"Think of your head!" Sam screamed.

"An alligator in the canal," Nana said. "I'm flabbergasted."

"They've got something," Jeep said.

"We told you there's an alligator," I said. "Look! They got its skin."

"Do alligators shed like snakes?" Sam asked.

"No," Jeep said.

The wranglers came closer. I saw what it was.

"A slimy, mossy, wilted, torn green trash bag," Officer Mathur said.

"Litter's worse than an alligator," Jeep said.

He led them to the trash cans. Nana, Sam, and I cut through the house to the front yard.

"We all make mistakes," Officer Polozie said.

"There was an alligator," I said.

"It swam away," Sam said.

"Do you get a lot of mistaken-identity calls?" Nana asked.

"Polozie had a doozie," Officer Mathur said.

I was so mad that I didn't even say "good rhyme."

"A guy insisted he saw a shark. It was a floating beach umbrella," Officer Polozie said. "So don't feel silly, kids."

"We don't," Sam said. "Because it was a real alligator."

"It looked like one at first glance," Officer Mathur said. "The bag's torn so it looks long. Air bubbles were trapped underneath."

"The trash bag has nothing to do with the alligator," I said.

"You were right to call, son," Officer Polozie said. "If it had been an alligator, reporting it would be your civic duty."

I liked the part about me being right and my duty. The rest made me steam.

"What's civic duty?" Sam asked.

"Things we do for our community," Nana said. "Like voting and keeping the neighborhood clean."

"Reporting alligators," Officer Mathur said.

She smiled at me like I was five.

"Jeep's pulled several trash bags out of the canal over the past few months," Nana said.

"It's my civic duty," Jeep said.

If you ask me, reporting an alligator is a lot bigger duty than catching a trash bag.

I figured I should finally write back to Lucy Rose. Since we were at the villa, I used the computer.

> Dear Lucy Rose, Jonique, and Pip,
>   We've had two alligator happen-ings. When we zip lined over the al-ligator pit, the big ones snapped their jaws and hissed at us. We had to pull our legs up for safety. Sam

and I also saw an alligator in the canal behind Nana and Jeep's house. Nana, Jeep, and the Wildlife Control people think we panicked over a floating trash bag. Can you believe it?

You have a good way of getting your grandparents to do what you want. Tell me your method before someone gets eaten. I'll check back to see your advice.

Melonhead and Sam

33

THE BEACH

"Let's pack our picnic so we're ready to go when Geoffrey and Mary Alice get here," Nana said.

"They're coming with us?" Sam asked.

"Maeve has a city council meeting," Jeep said.

"I'm surprised at you boys," Nana said. "You haven't reached out to Geoffrey."

"He says our ideas stink," I said.

"He shows off how smart he is," Sam said.

"Why do you think he does that?" Nana asked.

"To be annoying," I said.

"Put yourself in Geoffrey's loafers,"

Jeep said. "He doesn't know anyone here, except his aunt and his little sister."

"He's acting like that because he's hoping you'll want to be his friend," Nana said.

"By starting wars and showing off?" I said.

"We didn't say it was a good way to make friends," Nana said. "But it's the best way he knows. He's kind of an awkward kid."

"He's twelve," I said. "He can't be awkward."

"You two are a team," Nana said. "He wants to join."

When Jeep answered the doorbell, Mary Alice gave him handfuls of dead grass.

"Pauline, eat this hay every eight minutes or you'll get too weak!" she screeched.

"Where did you get this hay?" Jeep asked.

"From where I'm allowed to go," she said. "Chew it, Pauline. Or else there will be no donuts forever. Do you want no donuts forever?"

"I do not," Jeep said.

"Mary Alice, you can't make him eat grass," Geoffrey said.

Mary Alice ignored him.

"Pauline, tell me when eight minutes are over so you can eat more," she said.

"Mary Alice," Nana said, "can you carry the potato chips to the Melonmobile?"

"Sure I can," she said, and hugged the bag until the chips were potato dust.

"Geoffrey and Sam, carry the cooler," Jeep said. "I've got the blanket and towels."

"I'll get the lemonade jug," I said.

"Are we going by Melonmobile?" Geoffrey asked.

"Just to the parking lot," Nana said. "We'll drive our car to the beach."

"Is it a Meloncar?" Mary Alice asked.

"Not yet," Jeep said. "But I'm working on it."

Nana gave him a look.

Florida beaches aren't like Delaware beaches.

"The ocean's ultra-blue here," Sam said.

"It's bluer in Miami," Geoffrey said.

"Spread the quilt on the sand, boys," Nana said. "Mary Alice and I will set up a make-your-own sandwich station."

When Geoffrey saw the picnic table, he shouted, "It's a feast!"

He made a triple-decker sandwich with roast beef, cheese, hot pepper, tomato, ham, olive, lettuce, and artichoke hearts.

"Never in my life will I eat a heart," I said.

Mary Alice dipped a strawberry in mayonnaise.

"Here's your food, Pauline," she said.

"Let's make Pauline a sandwich," Nana said.

"Sandwiches make show ponies' throats get tangled and they feel very severe and have to take black medicine for eleven years. Right, Pauline?"

"That is severe," Jeep said.

Geoffrey gave his sister a bun.

"Smear the mayonnaise all over, Mary Alice," he said.

"Do not smear mayonnaise all over Mary Alice!" Mary Alice screeched.

I made her a ham roll-up.

"Where are the alligator nests?" Sam said.

"Alligators don't live in salt water," Geoffrey said.

"Good," I said.

"The boys thought they saw an alligator in the canal today," Nana said. "Thankfully, it was a trash bag."

"It was an alligator," I said.

"Now you're scared," Geoffrey said.

"Who wouldn't be?" Sam said. "It was twelve feet long."

"Or longer," I said.

Luckily, Geoffrey doesn't talk much when he's eating.

Sam and I handwalked until Jeep said to do something Geoffrey could do. We dug a moat. When it got washed away, we looked for starfish. Geoffrey found six shark teeth. Sam and I found zero. Even though Geoffrey can find them anytime, he didn't share.

Finally, Nana said we could swim. We stayed in

the ocean until Jeep gave the thirty-second warning. Then we rolled in the sand for fun and to hide our tantoos.

On the way home, I pretended I couldn't hear Geoffrey bragging about meeting a real astronaut whose footprints will stay on the moon for eternity because there's no wind in outer space.

Mary Alice was asleep on the purple sofa when their aunt Maeve came to get them.

Geoffrey carried her to their golf cart.

"If you want to check for more alligators, shine a flashlight on the canal," he said. "At night, their eyes glow red."

My brain was too full to listen to Jeep read Tom Swift. All I could think was: if we can't get the Distractor to work, Jeep and Nana are alligator bait.

In my mind, I made a tough choice. Then I fell asleep so hard I didn't hear the barking frogs.

*   *   *

When we woke up, we checked our emails.

Good morning, Melonhead and Sam,
    We say the Wild Animal Collectors
were right. Here's why:
    1. They are professionals.
    2. You have been wrong before, no
offense.
    3. How could an alligator get
through a wall?
    Don't forget our gift, please.
                        From,
                        Lucy Rose

P.S. The Excellent Thing is hard
work. Clue: it's something we are
making.

34

THE SACRIFICE

After breakfast, I told Nana and Jeep, "Sam and I have to Zip over to the Ponce."

"It doesn't open until nine," Jeep said.

"We're stopping off at Geoffrey's," Sam said.

"You've changed your opinion about him?" Jeep asked.

"Maybe," I said.

When Mary Alice saw us, she went berserk—if *berserk* is the word that means cuckoo.

"Is Geoffrey home?" I asked.

"Geoffrey!" Mary Alice called. "The chair boys are here."

"Really?" Geoffrey said.

I looked him square in his eyeballs.

"Geoffrey," I said. "Do you want to be on our team?"

"Yes," he said.

"Come on, then," Sam said.

"Don't forget me!" Mary Alice yelled.

"Mary Alice," Aunt Maeve said, "today is spa day. You get to paint my toenails."

"You can go away, chair boys!"

I called Nana from the sidewalk. Sam called when we got to the Ponce.

The only thing in the workroom was a lopsided birdhouse.

"Nothing to do but sit and wait," Geoffrey said.

"We never sit," I said.

"Or wait," Sam said.

"I vote we practice our secret agent skills," I said. "I'm the leader."

"Follow him, Geoffrey," Sam said. "Back to the wall."

I led them down a mystery hall. Mystery because we'd never been in it.

"Stop breathing, Geoffrey," I said. "They could hear you."

"Who are they?" Geoffrey asked.

"Shhh!" Sam and I said at the exact same time.

"The hall floor slopes," I whispered.

"Because they don't have steps in this building," Geoffrey said.

"Shh!" Sam and I told him again.

"When I give the signal, roll down," I said. "When you get to the end, jump around the corner, ninja-style."

Geoffrey rolled too soon. Sam and I went right after, but it's impossible to get ahead when you're rolling. Watching him roll while I was rolling was like flicking a light switch up and down from dark to light to dark. I caught flashes of him. On the last flash Geoffrey was in midair. His hands were curled like cat claws.

"Aha!" he screamed.

"Aaackkk!" someone else screamed.

A red-haired lady smashed dead into him.

I scraped my sneakers against the floor tile. It works like an emergency brake.

"Why are you jumping at me?" the lady squealed.

To be fair to Geoffrey, who knew somebody would be coming around the corner?

Sam rolled into me. My face hit Geoffrey's heel. When I looked up, Geoffrey was holding the lady up by her elbows.

"You're fine," I said to calm her.

"No harm, no foul," Sam said.

Right then her mini-dog leapt out of her arms and ran for freedom.

"Come back, Leroy!" she yelled.

"He's extremely fast for an animal with legs the size of French fries," I said.

"Catch him!" the lady yelled. "You are responsible for this."

That remark gave me confidence.

"You can count on us," I said.

"We've got spy skills!" Geoffrey yelled.

The three of us charged after Leroy.

"He's running into the Sunkist Demonstration Kitchen!" Sam shouted.

"Good news!" I yelled so the lady would know we had everything under control. "We have him cornered."

When I said it, I thought it was true. How could I know the room was full of people sitting in folding chairs and a man holding a giant fish over his head?

"Of all the places to have a cooking class," Sam said.

Leroy ran between people legs and chair legs.

"Is that a dog?" the chef shouted.

The whole room answered.

Leroy ran to the chef.

"Shoo!" the chef shouted. "Go away!"

Leroy hopped around on his hind legs.

People clapped.

"The dog wants the fish," someone said.

I didn't know dogs like fish, but they must, because Leroy was clawing the chef's checkered pants. The chef tried to shake him off. That's hard to do when your arms are holding a huge, wet fish. Luckily for the chef and the fish, dogs are terrible climbers.

Leroy started licking the chef's ankle.

The chef started laughing like a spotted hyena.

The audience laughed like a thousand spotted hyenas.

"That cured his mood," Sam said.

Wrong. The chef was ticklish. He couldn't help laughing. That made him madder.

"Bad dog! *Ha-ha-haaaa. Grrr.* Stop it! *Hee-haaa.* Go away. *Ha-har-he-ha huh.* Vamoose!"

He was holding the fish like a baby and kicking his feet.

"He looks like he's tap-dancing," Sam whispered.

His chef's hat hit the floor. A clog flew off. Leroy bit the end of his sock and pulled. The audience went hysterical. If *hysterical* is the word that means uncontrollable laughing.

Leroy wouldn't let go.

"Get the dog," Geoffrey said.

"Oh, right!" I said.

"Don't worry, Chef," Sam shouted. "Help is here!"

"Block him!" I yelled.

"The chef?" Geoffrey yelled.

"The dog!" the chef screamed.

It was hard to hear over the laughing.

For a split second, I nearly had him. Then I didn't.

"Whose dog is this?" the cook yelled. "He does not belong in the kitchen! He should be on a leash! Why is he here? Where is the owner? He is unclean."

"The owner's a lady," I said.

"The *dog* is unclean," the chef said.

I was closing in on Leroy when my foot landed on fish guts. For a second I felt like I was water-skiing. Then I was on my butt.

I didn't mean to kick the chef's legs. I'm pretty sure the chef didn't mean to drop the fish on me. I

know Leroy didn't mean to get
caught, but that's what happens when you stop to stick
your head in a lady's pocketbook.

I'd never heard adults laugh
that hard.

"*Get out!*" the chef shouted. "This is a class,
not a circus."

The dog-catching lady handed Leroy to Sam, who
carried him to the back of the room. I gave him to
the lady.

Her name was Fran Farmer.

"We saved your dog," I told her.

"*You* saved my dog?" she yelled.

"Yes," I said, louder, so she could
hear. "We *saved* your dog!"

Since my mom can't check
email unless she's at a café and
Sam's mom gets them the second
he hits send, I let him go first.

Dear Mom,

A lady lost her dog. We caught it and gave it back.

Love,
Sam

Dear Sam,

That lady must be grateful. I'm sure the dog appreciated being rescued. I told Julia that her brother is a hero. She growled.

Love,
Mom

Dear Mom,

It wasn't like that, but don't tell Julia that I'm not a hero. OK?

Love,
Sam

P.S. Geoffrey has improved about four percent.

Then I wrote to my mom.

Dear Mom,

You know the Melon Family Guideline Be Trustworthy? We must be, because Mrs. Farmer trusted us to

catch her runaway dog. She said we
were responsible.

But remember you said certain
adults need the Polite People Program? She's one of them. She didn't
say thanks.

Love,
Melonhead

Then I checked in with the girls.

Dear Lucy Rose, Pip, and Jonique,
About your great thing: does it
have to do with Baking Divas?

Melonhead and Sam

My mom answered me back in between.

DB,
What kind of woman tells children to chase a dog? It could have
been a biter. You could have gotten
a scar. Did you? Where were Nana and
Jeep?

I'm not surprised that she was
rude and unthankful. I wish I could
tell her what I think about that.

I love you,
Mom

Dear Mom,
    The dog's as big as a squirrel.
Nobody got bitten. Or scarred. Or
scared.
                    Love,
                    DB

35

EMERGENCY ANNOUNCEMENT

When we got to the workroom, Squinty was teaching a lady to glue on a roof. Not a real roof. A birdhouse roof, luckily, because she was not learning much.

"Meet my wife," Squinty said.

"Hello, Mrs. Squinty," Sam said.

"Call me Greta," she said. "Or Mrs. Squinty. That's new, but I like it."

"Remember Geoffrey?" Sam said. "He's helping us."

"Before we start, we have to do a civic duty," I said. "There's danger in Paradise."

Everybody was staring at me. I felt like I was Congressman Buddy Boyd.

"There's an alligator in the canal," I said. "It's gigantic."

Everybody talked over everybody.

"Our canal?"

"There are no alligators in Paradise."

"Is there a hole in the underwater fence?"

"Where was the gator?"

"Swimming behind my grandparents' house," I said.

"Did the wranglers come?"

"They said it was a trash bag," Sam said. "And Melonhead's grandparents believed them."

"A trash bag! That's a relief."

"You frightened me."

"Light played tricks on your eyes."

"Our eyes weren't tricked," I said. "Nana and Jeep need protection."

"Everybody in Paradise needs protection," Sam said.

"But my grandparents come first," I said. "No offense."

"Did you figure out how to get the marshmallow to fly a good distance?" Mr. Thompson asked.

"Nope," I said. "That's why we brought Geoffrey."

It stung my tongue to admit it.

Geoffrey looked at the Distractor from all sides.

"We need a bicycle tire pump," he said.

"I volunteer with Coach Mac's wife," Mrs. Squinty said. "I'll run over and borrow one from her."

"That's a Brainflash of Brilliance," I said.

It was a fast trip.

"Coach Mac says it's old, so you can keep it," she said.

Geoffrey hooked it up in a flash.

I didn't think his plan would work but, due to being polite, I didn't say it out loud.

"Everybody who wants to try the Distractor, pick a partner. It takes two people to Distract," Sam said.

"Follow Sam and me to the Johnny Depp Terrace," I said. "Also follow Geoffrey."

We unloaded our pockets and let Geoffrey pass out the marshmallows. Mine were covered with ants.

Mrs. Squinty and Mrs. Fontaine did a test launch without permission.

"Eight feet, one inch," Mrs. Fontaine said.

"Hotpachonga!" Sam screamed. "It works!"

I made a rule.

"Youngest first," I said.

My marshmallow went nine feet, four inches. Sam got thirteen feet, one inch. Geoffrey got nine feet exactly. The winner was Mr. Thompson. He got eighteen feet, eleven inches.

"The angle is important," Mr. Thompson said. "Point up and the marshmallow will fall short. Point too low, it'll hit the dirt."

"He knows," I told Geoffrey. "He's a rocket engineer."

"That's what I'm going to be," Geoffrey said.

The second round was better.

"Why are you guys laughing so much?" Sam asked.

"We're having fun," Squinty said.

"You should have been in the cooking class," I told him. "Those people couldn't stop laughing."

Mrs. Fontaine broke our invention.

"It's a quick fix," Squinty said. "We tested it before the glue dried. Reglue it and leave it here until tomorrow."

"We have to keep my grandparents inside tonight," I said.

"This Distractor is NASA-worthy," Mr. Thompson said.

Sam, Geoffrey, and I did a six-hand high-five.

"That's the greatest praise an inventor can get," I said.

We let Geoffrey pick up the marshmallows.

36

EMBARRASSED TIMES INFINITY

Geoffrey pushed Zippy. Sam rode. I followed.

"You know why nobody believes we saw an alligator?" I said. "Because we're kids."

"I believe you," Geoffrey said.

"Ditto," Sam said.

"Of course you believe, Sam," I said. "You saw it. But Geoffrey believes us out of friendship."

That was a blurt.

"I was unsticking the door," Sam said.

"After you saw the alligator," I said.

"I heard you scream 'Alligator!'" Sam said.

"Then you saw it," I said.

Sam's forehead wrinkled.

"A lot was going on," he said. "My mind was screaming 'Run!' And I did."

"You didn't see the alligator?" I asked.

"I couldn't have," Sam said. "You had the binoculars."

"But you said, 'Nana, you should've seen it.'"

"She should have," Sam said. "She's the one who lives here."

"You told the officers it was twelve feet long," I said.

"That's what you told me," he said. "I believe you."

"Just because he didn't see an alligator doesn't mean it wasn't there," Geoffrey said. "I don't see things all the time."

I saw the truth.

"Everybody's right," I said. "It was a garbage bag. I feel ridiculous."

"It's an easy mistake," Sam said. "And you thought it was real, so it's still a civic duty."

"I was only worrying about us," I said. "And Nana and Jeep. I didn't think of the community. Or you, Geoffrey. No offense."

"None taken," he said.

"If it was real, you would've been the hero who saved me," Sam said.

"I'm a chump," I said.

"I'm relieved," Sam said.

"My mom says everyone learns from mistakes," Geoffrey said.

"That's a Melon Family Motto too," I said.

I did not expect that people who let their child have two dogs would have the same Guidelines as us Melons.

Sam made us stop at Parrot Kingdom. The parrots ignored us. I didn't care.

"Parrots stay away from people," Geoffrey said.

"Not pirates," I said.

"Pirates didn't have pet parrots," Geoffrey said. "People got that idea from reading *Treasure Island*."

"You do know a lot," I said.

"I hope the armadillo doesn't fail us," Sam said.

```
Hi.
    Jeep and Nana took us to Ripley's
Believe It or Not Museum. Do you be-
lieve it? Or not?
```

The most exciting thing is there's
a tunnel that has lights and mirrors
and you can't find your way out. It
makes you feel like you're going to
throw up. We went through it FIVE
times. Jeep went once. Nana zero. She
doesn't like feeling dizzy.

When I'm an inventor and Sam's a
professional baseball player, we're
also going to be collectors for Rip-
ley's Odditorium.

Melonhead and Sam

We emailed the same letter to everybody so we
didn't have to redo it. I almost wrote to Lucy Rose,
Jonique, and Pip to admit I was wrong about the alligator, but we decided they didn't need to know every
detail of our lives. It was a false alarm, and like my
dad says, mistakes happen.

Sam remembered to check for emails.

DB,
Nana wrote me. She said you and
Sam are the best guests they ever
had. I think that includes me. It's
nice in Vermont, but I miss you, of
course.

I'm bringing home a jug of maple

syrup. Daddy can make us his famous buckwheat pancakes.

Your proud mom

Dear Mom,

I can help with pancakes. Tonight I cooked pizza! Jeep said I'm smart enough not to leave my arm in the oven, so he let me slide the pan in. I yanked my hand back fast. The door didn't slam on my arm. I did not get burned. Cooking is fun.

Love,
DB

Sam got mail too.

Dear Sam,

Good news! Oliver and Daddy finally got pictures of the yellow-haired woolly monkey. They're coming home late tonight. Julia and I are driving home tomorrow morning. We can't wait to hug you both.

Miss and love you,
Mom

37

WORKING AT MIDNIGHT

*U*nless it's Christmas Eve, staying awake is hard.

We read Tom Swift and played flashlight tag on the ceiling. Sam made up a song about armadillos. Luckily, the Barking Tree Frogs are like an all-night alarm.

Finally, it was midnight.

"Up and Adam," Sam said. That expression is the only time he calls me my birth certificate name.

We found an empty box in the garage, crept around the side of the house, and shined a flashlight into the bucket.

Bugs ran every which way.

"High five, Clive!" Sam rhymed.

"Extreme success, Jess," I said.

"Set up the trap in the back of the front yard, in between the yuccas," Sam said. "Otherwise the armadillo could see it and get spooked."

We balanced one side of the box on a stick. I put a pile of Armadillo Attractor underneath.

"He goes in for food. His butt hits the stick. The box falls. And it's hello, pet," I said.

We dropped handfuls of Attractor in lines. They all led to the box.

"This is one of our most brilliant ideas," I said.

"It better work," Sam said. "Or I'm going home with nothing."

"In the last minute of the fourth quarter, you will get a pet," I said. "I know it."

"Nana and Jeep will be mega-surprised when there's an armadillo at the breakfast table," Sam said.

"And delighted," I said.

38

THE DISASTER

Sam and I were dead asleep when we heard the screams.

Jeep ran past our door, yelling, "Hold on, Doll! I'm coming!"

"We're all coming!" I shouted.

The front door was open. Nana was standing on the fish mat.

"Are you hurt, Doll?" Jeep asked.

"No," Nana said. "But look."

I could not believe it.

"Who did this?" I shouted.

"What kind of person sneaks in and wrecks somebody's yard?" I said. "And knocks over their Miami Dolphins flamingo?"

"Whoever did this is in a load of trouble," Sam said.

"This is the work of armadillos," Jeep said.

I felt like my ears were full of honey. "What?"

The box was still leaning on the stick.

"Why would armadillos dig up your yard?" Sam asked.

"They were looking for bugs," Nana said.

"There were hundreds of bugs, right there, in the grass," I said.

"Maybe thousands," Sam said. "They didn't need to dig."

I stared at my bare feet. Sam looked at the sky.

"Women who raise three sons develop boy radar," Nana said. "Mine is going off."

"Your radar's faulty, Doll. The boys didn't do this."

"We're a little responsible," I admitted.

"For your age you're quite responsible," Jeep said.

"He means a little responsible for the yard," Sam said.

"But it's mostly the armadillos' fault," I said.

"Mostly?" Nana asked.

"And a little bit Jeep's," I said.

"My fault?" Jeep asked.

"You're the one who said bugs like fruit," I said. "That's the top ingredient in Armadillo Attractor."

"You enticed armadillos into our yard?" Jeep asked. "On purpose?"

"If *entice* means lure, yes," I said.

"Why?" Nana asked.

"I promised Sam he'd go home with a pet," I said.

"We wasted a ton of time on parrots," Sam said. "And alligators."

Nana's eyes popped.

"A pet armadillo?" she said.

Sam nodded.

"Now you can see the problem," I said.

"Everyone can see the problem," Nana said.

She meant the yard. I meant Sam's going home petless.

"Nobody told us armadillos are yard destroyers," Sam said.

"If you'd told us your plan, we would've told you

that armadillos are like small, runaway plows," Jeep said.

"We'll fix up your yard," I said. "For free."

"I'm torn between being angry and admiring their curiosity and resourcefulness," Jeep said to Nana.

"I'm not torn," Nana answered.

I did not know that she could do the Xtreme Laser Glare.

"Once armadillos find food, they return," Nana said. "I don't know what to do about that."

"I do," I said.

I ran inside, found the "People in Paradise" booklet, and called for a rescue. I also got Jeep's safari hat so his head wouldn't fry.

We raked shredded grass and stomped roots back into holes.

"We should water the spots," Jeep said.

39

THE ACCIDENTAL REVEAL

Nana went inside and came back with two bars of soap.

"Lather up," she said. "Heads to toes."

Jeep sprayed us.

"This is my kind of shower," I said.

After five minutes Nana said, "Clean enough."

"Why are your faces two-tone?" Jeep asked.

Tantoos!

I looked at Sam. "You look like you got smacked in the face with a bat," I said. "Bat the mammal. Not baseball."

"Your bolts are outstanding," Sam said.

"What happened?" Nana asked.

"It didn't just happen," I said. "We made it happen."

"They're tantoos," Sam explained. "Melonhead invented them."

"All it takes is sun and sunblock," I said.

"So there's no chance this will wash off?" Nana asked.

"That's the great part," I told her. "But it will disappear when the suntan wears off."

"Whose tantoo is more likeable?" Sam asked.

"They're both atrocious," Nana said.

"Good," I said. "I'd be disappointed if you didn't like them."

We were drying off when a golf cart pulled into the driveway.

"I hear you survived an armadillo attack," the driver said.

"Who's that?" Nana whispered to Jeep.

"It's Mr. Clarke," I said. "He's had experience with armadillos."

"Your grandson called me for help," Mr. Clarke said.

"Any advice?" Jeep asked. "We don't want our yard to become a regular stop on the armadillo tour."

"I'm afraid you're not going to like my answer," Mr. Clarke said. "The only solution is putting up a fence."

"I love your answer!" Nana exclaimed.

Jeep didn't, but he said he could live with a fence better than he could live with armadillos.

"It has to be a wooden picket fence. No spaces between the boards," Mr. Clarke explained. "And it has to be white. Paradise rules."

"Nana," I said. "That was your lucky armadillo."

She was perking up.

"I brought chicken wire and metal posts," Mr. Clarke said.

"Wait a minute," Sam interrupted. "Do they have wild chickens in Florida?"

"Only in Key West," Mr. Clarke answered. "They walk around town."

"You're not getting a chicken, Sam," Nana declared.

"We can put up a temporary fence," Mr. Clarke said.

"I'll get my tools," Jeep announced.

"I'll get limeade," Nana said.

"Sam and I will help," I added.

Then Mr. Clarke complimented Jeep. "I'm a big fan of your Melonmobile."

"She's a beauty, isn't she?" Jeep declared.

Since it was too late for breakfast, Nana invited Mr. Clarke for lunch. Mr. Clarke invited Jeep to go golfing Tuesday morning.

"I'll pick you up in the Melonmobile," Jeep said.

Sam and I were carrying the plates inside when I heard Mr. Clarke ask Jeep, "What happened to their faces?"

"You know how it is with inventors," Jeep said.

That made me feel smart.

*   *   *

I sent my mom email from the Ernest Hemingway Center.

> Dear Mom,
>   You were right about Nana and Jeep needing rest. Yard work wore them out. Sam and I just picked up our invention. Now we're going to look at parrots. We have spare energy.
>   Love,
>   Melonhead

> DB,
>   Do *NOT* touch a parrot. You don't know where it's been.
>   Love,
>   Mom

40

A GREAT THING HAPPENS

We were burpspeaking the alphabet when Sam let go of Zippy and I landed in somebody's yard.

When I got up, a parrot was walking up Sam's arm.

"Hi, bird," Sam said.

"You did it!" I whispered. "You found a pet!"

The bird stood on Sam's head, pulling his hair out with its beak.

"Hair makes a good nest," I said.

"Awrk!" the bird said.

"Awrk!" Sam answered.

The parrot took off.

"Come back!" I yelled.

It landed on a palm tree.

Then it flew back to Sam.

"I'm naming him Buster," Sam said.

"Good name."

In case Buster was scared of rolling noises, I carried Zippy back to the villa. Sam carried the Distractor. Buster rode on Sam.

Nana saw us from the yard.

"Sam!" Nana said. "There's a bird on your head."

Buster flew to Nana's head.

She covered her face.

"Shoo, bird," she said.

"Come here, bird," Sam said. And Buster did.

"Buster's tame," Jeep said.

"Thanks to Sam," I said.

"He's a fast learner," Sam said.

"Put Buster in the sunroom until we figure out what to do," Nana said.

Nana covered the chairs with sheets. Jeep looked up parrots' diets.

"They enjoy peanut butter, walnuts, kale, and carrots," Jeep said.

We made Buster lunch on a paper plate.

"This is my luckiest day," Sam said.

"Not mine," I said. "I figured out I was wrong about the alligator."

"Alligators are a good thing to be wrong about," Jeep said.

"Is this thing your Distractor?" Jeep asked.

"How did you make such a fancy machine?" Nana asked.

"We drew plans," Sam said.

"Geoffrey helped," I said.

"If Einstein were here, his self-esteem would shrivel up," Nana said.

"It's no good here, but you can take it with you when you visit the Everglades," I said.

"You don't mean we can keep it?" Nana said.

"We do mean that," Sam said.

"Tom Swift would be jealous," Jeep said.

41

BACK AT THE BUFFET

We spent the afternoon at the pool playing Marco Polo with Jeep. Only the person who was it shouted "Ponce." And the others shouted "De León." Then I shouted "Major BOB!" which was confusing.

"What's your Brainflash of Brilliance?" Sam asked.

"Let's eat dinner at the buffet," I said.

"Excellent brainflash," Jeep said.

We went home so Nana could put on her green dress and gold shoes. Jeep wore a Hawaiian shirt, red shorts, Happy Socks, and sandals. Sam and I wore what we always wear.

"I'm surrounded by handsome men," Nana said.

We parked the Melonmobile in the Young People's Lot and walked in with Mr. Clarke.

"The joint is jumping tonight," Jeep said.

"Hey, Mr. Thompson," I yelled.

"He's a rocket scientist," Sam told Nana.

"I've enjoyed getting to know these boys," Mr. Thompson said.

"You'll enjoy getting to know Nana and Jeep even more," I said. "They're better than we are."

"Hi, Lovey!" Sam yelled.

Lovey rushed over and squeezed Nana's hand.

"I love your Happy Socks, Jeep!" she said.

"You know about my Happy Socks?" Jeep asked.

"We know a lot about you," Squinty said.

"Oh, dear," Nana said.

"There's Joe," I said.

"Hello, kids," he said.

"The Squintys moved here from Brooklyn, New York," I said. "He was in the garment business. That's the same as clothes."

"I'm Greta," Mrs. Squinty said.

"I'm Carol Melon. People call me Doll."

"Do you play tennis, Jeep?" Squinty asked.

"Not well," Jeep said.

"Me either," Squinty said. "Meet me at the courts at noon on Monday. We'll see who's worse."

Three ladies with puffy hair walked over.

"Who are they?" Nana asked.

"Strangers," I said.

"Are you related to the dogcatchers?" one asked Nana.

Nana looked at Jeep like he had a relative she didn't know about.

"We're the dogcatchers," I told Nana.

"These boys had us laughing so hard we got hiccups," she said.

"I thought I'd die when the chef dropped a fish on him," the middle one told them.

"I had no idea," Nana said.

"We're Tina, Terri, and Madge," the last one said. "We're sisters."

Mrs. Fontaine leaned over the salad bar to shake hands with Nana and Jeep.

"I've been told you need friends," she said. "Stick with me. I know everybody."

"Come country line dancing Friday night," Lovey said.

"I'm as flat-footed as a duck," Jeep said. "But Doll's spectacular."

"I'll bet you're relieved to have an Alligator Distractor," Squinty said to Jeep.

Jeep laughed. "We're well protected."

"That's the boy who was running around outside in his underwear!" someone yelled.

My face turned Twizzler red.

"Is she talking about you?" Nana whispered.

"Ants in his pants," Sam explained so I wouldn't have to answer.

Mr. Thompson was taking Nana and Jeep to meet his friend when somebody squealed.

"Pauline!" Mary Alice screamed. "You got out of your corral!"

"This young lady is my veterinarian," Jeep told Mrs. Fontaine. "She cured me."

"That sickness is done," Mary Alice said. "Now your legs feel bendy. I have to cover them with wet napkins."

"Want to sit with Sam and me?" I asked Geoffrey.

"Sure," he said. "Aunt Maeve, you and Mary Alice can sit with Nana and Jeep."

The adults at the big table did not stop laughing, talking, or eating until Ms. Fadul said, "It's closing time."

"I'll sign us out," Jeep said.

Sam and I were shocked when Jeep told us that For the Convenience of the Residents doesn't mean free.

42
I WISH WE NEVER SAW IT

Since Jeep and Nana were in the front of the Melon-mobile, they didn't see the sign. Sam and I were riding backwards, so we did.

ESCAPED PARROT
Mostly Green
Friendly!
Name: MAYBELLE.
Please call Virginia BLISS

I jabbed Sam's ribs.

"Buster's wild," Sam said.

"He's mostly green," I whispered.

At home, Sam and I went to the bird room.

"Maybelle," Sam whispered.

"Maybelle," I said in a normal voice.

"Awrk," the parrot squawked.

Sam smiled. "He's not Maybelle."

"That's a relief," I said.

"Maybelle," the bird said.

"That doesn't mean he's Maybelle," Sam said. "It means he's smart. He's copying us."

"Pretty girl. Wanna dance?"

The bird picked up one claw, put it down, and picked up the other.

"It talks better than it dances," I said.

"Say *Sam*," Sam said.

"Pretty girl."

"Sam," Sam said. "Sam, Sam, Sam, Sam."

"Maybelle," it said.

"I think she's Maybelle," I told Sam.

"I want her to be Buster," he said.

"Maybelle wanna dance," Maybelle said.

"Say *fart*, Maybelle," I said.

"Fart, fart, fart, fart," Sam said.

"Say *fart*," I begged.

"Pretty girl," Maybelle said.

We said *fart* over a hundred times. Maybelle didn't copy us.

Nana found Mrs. Bliss's phone number in "People in Paradise." Sam left a message.

43
PANIC

"Who wants to help me weed the backyard?" Jeep asked. "We have time before sunset."

"Who wants to help me do the laundry?" Nana said.

"No thanks," Sam said.

"He's down in the dumps," I said. "About Buster being Maybelle."

"Chin up, Sam," Nana said. "We'll play Uno after I've turned on the washing machine and taken a bath."

"I wish you'd stop bathing in the washing machine," Jeep said. "There's no room for clothes."

Sam laughed.

"Music can cure your blues, Sam," Jeep said. "Sing along with me, Ray Charles, and the Raelettes."

"No thanks," Sam said.

"More music for me," Jeep said.

He pushed earbuds into his canals. Ear canals. Not the water. That would ruin them.

"We didn't get a present for the girls yet," Sam said. "We should have built an extra Distractor."

"Idea alert," I said. "We'll give them a video of us playing with the Distractor."

"They won't be thankful," Sam said.

"We'll put drama in it," I said.

"They will like drama," Sam said.

"Jeep's singing can be background music," I said. "Set his phone to record. Put it where it won't get beaned with marshmallows."

"Deal-E-O," Sam said.

"I'll get the Distractor," I said. "And costumes."

Sam put on Jeep's orange and blue sunhat and a cape made out of a Christmas apron. I wore Nana's yellow bathing cap and stuffed a torn-up paper bag under it for hair. Our tantoos made us look excellent.

I rested the front of the Distractor on the top of the deck railing.

"I'll load," I said. "You work the pump. I'll aim. You turn the knob."

The marshmallow bounced off Jeep's butt.

"He didn't notice," I said.

"Jeep!" Sam hollered.

"He turned the volume too high," I said. "He can't hear over the music."

"And his own singing," Sam said.

The next marshmallow landed a foot from Jeep's foot.

"Reload, Toad," I said.

Nothing.

I turned around.

 Sam's mouth was in the scream position without any sound.

He pointed.

"Oh, my sweet potato," I said. "This is the worst."

A monster alligator was climbing

out of the canal. This one was real. And big. Its claws tore the dirt. It walked across the grass swinging its tail. It looked at Jeep.

My stomach felt like a rubber-band ball.

"It sees the marshmallows!" Sam cried.

"I've never been this scared in my life," I said.

44
TRYING TO SAVE JEEP

I tried shouting. "Jeeeep! An alligator! Behind you! Move!!!"

Sam screamed, "Run, Jeep!"

Jeep was on his knees, pulling weeds and throwing them over his shoulder. And still singing his lungs out.

"Jeeeeeep!" I shouted. "Please move!"

"Jeeeeeep!" Sam yelled.

Jeep's butt wiggles when he sings. "Geoffrey said alligators are attracted to movement," I said.

"And Happy Socks," Sam said.

"Nana!" I yelled.

"Nobody can hear us," Sam said.

The alligator swung his head and stared at us. Jaws opened.

"Sharp teeth," Sam said.

"Yelling could make it mad," I whispered. "We have to save Jeep."

Finally, I got the obvious idea.

"Launch the Distractor," I said.

"You're shaking," Sam whispered.

"I should aim to the left of the gator," I said. "Right?"

"Right," Sam said. "Right like correct. Aim left. Away from Jeep."

"We have one chance," I said.

"We have a few chances," Sam said. "Be calm."

Sam pumped fast.

"I'm aiming," I said. "Turn the knob."

The marshmallow curved across the yard. The gator moved closer to Jeep.

"Should I get Nana?" Sam asked.

"No," I said. "I can't work the Distractor without you."

"Reload," Sam said.

"Launch," I said.

My aim was better, but the gator wasn't distracted.

"What if this is the only gator that hates marsh-mallows?" I said.

I aimed too low. The marshmallow landed in front of the alligator.

The alligator hissed.

"Please eat it," I whispered.

The alligator opened his jaws like it was going to swallow a sofa.

45
THE WORST MINUTES OF MY LIFE

"Why doesn't Jeep feel its breath on his foot?" I said.

"Aim for his teeth," Sam said.

"What if I miss?" I said. "What if it lands on Jeep?"

I wiped my eyes with my wrist.

The marshmallow flew over the alligator's snout and rolled over its right front leg.

The gator stepped on it.

"It didn't notice it," I said.

"Make a marshmallow trail to the canal," Sam said.

I reloaded. Sam repumped.

"Launch," I said.

The alligator turned toward the white spot.

"Did he eat it?" Sam asked.

"Ignored it," I said.

We launched another.

"Holy moly! He caught it!" I said.

The gator lifted his head, opened his mouth, and hissed.

"Yikes," I said.

I made myself stop shaking.

"Concentrate," Sam said.

The marshmallow flew over the yard and landed near the water.

The alligator snapped his jaws around it.

"Relaunch," I whispered.

"It's floating," Sam said.

The gator went for it.

My knees were slapping against each other.

"You did it!" Sam shouted. "You saved Jeep!"

"We did it," I said. "Let's get him inside."

When I got near Jeep, my noodle legs buckled. I landed on his back.

Sam jerked Jeep's earbuds.

Jeep turned his head fast. He looked mad.

"You scared me," he said.

"*We* scared you?" I said. "There was an ALLIGA-TOR!!!!"

"It was after your socks," Sam said.

"You know the story about the boy who cried wolf?" Jeep asked. "You are the boys who cry alligator. What if a real alligator showed up? You'd scream and no one would believe you."

"Believe us," I said.

"It was a huge nuisance," Sam said.

Jeep looked aggravated.

"Look!" I said. "It flattened the grass. That's proof."

"You boys have gone to a lot of trouble to prank me," he said.

The back door slid open and Nana came out. She was wearing her light blue bathrobe.

"Call the wranglers!" I shouted.

"The Distractor saved him," Sam said. "But now the gator knows where to get marshmallows."

Nana laughed. "I'm going to miss you two," she said. "It's lively when you're here. But not one more word about alligators."

46

MRS. BLISS

Nana knocked on our door.

"Wake up!" Nana said. "Mrs. Bliss called. She's coming to get her parrot."

I put on my FBI shirt and my cargo shorts.

"Hey, my pockets aren't sticky," I said.

"I can't send you home with tantoos and filthy clothes," Nana said. "I did your laundry while you were sleeping."

The doorbell buzzed.

Mrs. Bliss rushed to the sunroom.

Maybelle crash-landed in Mrs. Bliss's hairdo and pecked her scalp.

"I've missed my birdie kisses," Mrs. Bliss said in a birdish voice.

"Pretty girl," Maybelle said.

Mrs. Bliss opened her pocketbook and pulled out a tan clump of seedy weeds.

"Who wants millet?" she asked.

"Not me," I said.

Maybelle swooped down and grabbed a hunk of seeds.

"Oh, I was a soggy mess of tears until I got your message, Sam," Mrs. Bliss said.

"Wanna dance?" Maybelle squawked.

"Maybelle's lucky she found a good friend. Aren't you, Maybelle?" Mrs. Bliss said.

She got out a wad of money.

"For you, Sam."

"That's OK," Sam said. "I'm glad Maybelle has a nice owner."

"It's dog money," I whispered.

"Use it for something that makes you as happy as Maybelle makes me," Mrs. Bliss said.

Sam looked at Nana.

"You earned it," Nana said. "You took good care of Maybelle. Good work."

"Twenty-five dollars!" Sam shouted. "That's half a dog!"

I hooted. Maybelle flew up to the curtain rod.

I waved the millet.

"Who's a pretty girl?" Sam said.

"Pretty girl," Maybelle said. "Wanna dance?"

She landed on Mrs. Bliss's arm and leaned in like she was going to give her another beak kiss. Instead she spoke.

"Wanna fart, pretty girl?"

47
LEAVING

My dad came for us during breakfast. After hugs, he got a bagel and sat down.

"What's on your faces?" he asked

"Tantoos," Sam said. "Don't we look amazing?"

"That you do," my dad said.

"Jeep says we'll start a fad," I said.

"He's often right," my father said.

"Thanks to us, Nana's getting a fence," Sam said.

"Thanks to you?" my dad said.

"If it weren't for the boys, we wouldn't be getting it," Jeep said. "That's a fact."

"Sam's half responsible," I said. "And I'm half responsible."

"Jim Clarke already ordered the wood," Nana said.

"Jim Clarke?" my dad asked.

"Jeep's new golfing buddy," Nana said. "Jim's lady friend and I are having lunch while they play. Maeve says I'll like her."

"Who's Maeve?" my dad asked.

"My new friend," Nana said.

"You have friends?" my dad asked.

"Lots of them," Jeep said.

"Due to us," I said.

"Fantastic!" my dad said, smiling.

"And we saved Jeep from an alligator," Sam said.

"In his own backyard," I said.

My dad's eyes popped.

"The boys set up an elaborate trick," Jeep said. "They claim an alligator was inches from my toes, but somehow I didn't notice it."

"Because you were singing and weeding," I said.

"I would not overlook an alligator," Jeep said.

"The boys made us a fine Alligator Distractor," Nana said. "I think they were eager to use it."

"It worked," I said.

"Don't beat a joke to death, Sport," my dad said.

"Nana and Jeep are in danger," I said. "Believe me."

We heard the front door swing open.

"Probably another alligator," Jeep joked.

"It's me! Mary Alice. Plus Geoffrey. We're visiting you."

"Come in the kitchen," Nana said.

Mary Alice was wearing a yellow dress and socks on her hands.

"Aunt Maeve said come over because the chair boys are going home. Right, Geoffrey?"

"Right," Geoffrey mumbled.

Mary Alice walked up to my dad. "You can't look at Pauline unless you have a ticket. If you don't have a ticket, you have to keep your eyes closed. That's the law."

"That sounds fair," my dad said. "Who's Pauline?"

She put her hands on her hips and said, "Don't kid around, mister."

"Dad," I said, "Geoffrey's the one who got the Distractor working."

"You and Sam did most of it," Geoffrey said. "I came in at the end."

"Are you packed, Sport?" my dad asked.

"Thanks for letting me be on your team," Geoffrey said.

"I'm glad we let you," Sam said.

"It was the best choice I ever made," I added.

I had a big BOB.

"Wait for us in the driveway, Geoffrey," I said.

"Are you going to sneak up and throw oranges at me?" he asked.

It was the first time I saw him laugh.

Sam and I opened the garage from the inside.

"Keep it," Sam said.

"You're giving me Zippy?" Geoffrey said. "Why?"

"You're our friend," I said.

"I'm your friend," Mary Alice said.

"That's why we're giving you this pin," Sam said. "Airplane pilots wear them when they fly a plane."

"Hip-hooray!" she said. "I can drive a plane."

We hugged Nana and Jeep in the driveway.

"Dad, Mom, you're the best," my dad said. "Betty and I are grateful, and my boss thanks you. It'll be a close race but I think he'll win."

"Thanks for letting me come," Sam said.

"Our pleasure," Nana said.

We were backing out when Jeep hollered, "Stop!"

I leaned out the window.

"Do you have my phone?" Jeep asked.

"Oops," I said.

Sam jumped out. "I'll get it."

I ran after him. Everybody followed me.

"I hope it's not busted," Sam said. "I left it on the windowsill all night."

Nana plugged in the charger.

"It works," she said. "Were you making a movie?"

"I forgot about that," I said.

"Let's go, boys," my dad said.

I couldn't breathe.

Nana laughed. "You're wearing my bathing cap."

"Fast-forward," I said.

"That's me holding the Distractor," Sam said.

"And me singing," Jeep said.

"You're aiming the Distractor at Jeep's behind?" my dad asked.

"Keep watching," I said.

"What's that on the grass?" Jeep asked.

"The alligator," I said.

Nana went pale.

"It's crawling toward Jeep," she said.

"I estimate it weighs nine hundred pounds," Geoffrey said.

"It's inches from my foot," Jeep said. "Its mouth is wide open!"

His skin went pale.

Nana's breath shuddered.

"Don't worry," I said. "You know how it turns out."

"You're the bravest boys I've ever known," Jeep said. "Thank goodness you're OK."

"We were scared out of our heads," I said.

"Of course you were," Jeep said. "That's why it was brave."

Nana leaned against Jeep. She was crying.

We watched the alligator follow a marshmallow into the canal.

"That's why torn bags have been in the canal," Jeep said. "It's been crawling into yards and stealing garbage."

"And letting raccoons get the blame," Sam said.

When Jeep hugged Sam and me, I could feel his heart beating through his shirt.

My dad said, "I'm so grateful for you boys and the Alligator Distractor."

"That includes Geoffrey," I said.

"I don't have much courage," Geoffrey said.

"You might," I said. "You just haven't found out yet."

"I'm glad you talked us out of the egg," Sam said.

"What egg?" Nana asked.

"We have to send the video to Lucy Rose, Pip, and Jonique," I said. "We were making it for them."

"It's got drama," Sam said.

"Also email it to us," I said. "In case somebody doesn't believe us."

"There are people like that," Jeep said.

Everybody laughed.

Jeep and Nana hugged us so tight their arms felt like lassos.

When Dad was backing up, Nana yelled, "I'm calling the wranglers right now."

I yelled out the window, "Tell them Sam and I said we told you so."

We waved until we couldn't see them anymore.

On the plane ride home Sam said, "Melonhead, I decided something."

"What?"

"My dog's going to be our dog that lives at my house. We'll pick it out together and take care of it together. If we ever have another WOW, maybe your dad will let it stay in your room."

"This is the greatest thing that ever happened to me," I said. "And you're the greatest friend."

"You still have to pick up half the poop," Sam said.

My mom and dad, Sam's parents, and Julia met us at the airport.

My mom grabbed me into a hug so fast she didn't give me time to show her my tantoo. Sam got all the glory until she let go of my rib cage. At first, it seemed like she didn't like my lightning bolts.

"He's safe and sound," my dad said. "And tantoos don't last forever."

"They sort of will," I said. "Because school pictures are next week."

"And they're on our Lifetime List of Accomplishments," Sam said.

We took the metro to the Eastern Market stop.

"Lola McBee called as I was leaving," Mrs. Alswang said. "She said Lucy Rose, Pip, and Jonique are desperate to see our boys. I said we'd stop by for lunch on the walk home."

"Good thing we bought baby palm trees for them at the airport," I said.

But when we got there, Lucy Rose didn't ask for her present.

"We emailed you a movie we made," Sam said. "Did you get it?"

"We haven't looked at our mail yet," she said.

"Then why are you guys so excited?" I asked.

Pip passed Sam a little Baking Diva bag.

"Open it!" Jonique screamed.

Lucy Rose was tapping the toes of her red cowgirl boots so fast it sounded like Morse code.

Sam looked in the bag.

"Is it Banana Pockets?" I asked.

"There must be thirteen dollars in here," Sam said.

"For the dog fund," Lucy Rose said. "And don't worry, Mr. and Mrs. Alswang, we earned it."

"While we were gone?" I asked. "How?"

Then I spotted the new sign.

"'Junior Divas Biscuits for Good Dogs,'" Sam read. "Are you the Juniors?"

"The girls came up with the idea and invented a recipe," Mrs. McBee said. "It was such a success I bought it from them for twenty-five dollars."

"We kept half and gave you half," Lucy Rose said.

"That's the nicest thing ever!" I said.

"Does this count, Dad?" Sam asked. "Since I didn't earn it?"

"It counts," Mr. Alswang said. "Only a responsible, committed person would have such responsible, generous friends."

"Only four dollars and fifty-eight cents to go," Sam said.

Jonique opened the jar on the counter and gave Sam and me each a dog biscuit.

"Smells OK," Sam said.

"Tastes great," I said.

My mother gasped. "You ate it!"

"Sure," I said. "How else can we know if it's good enough for a dog?"

FLORIDA WILDLIFE CONTROL

Dear Adam and Sam,

Thank you for alerting us about the alligator in Paradise. It took our officers two days to locate him and two hours to wrangle him. We believe he came over the muddy banks into Paradise after the storms last spring. Once in the canal he dug in—literally—and stayed.

He's now the star of an Arkansas zoo. They named him Sam Adams after the boys who discovered him.

Enclosed are two Certificates for Meritorious Service, suitable for framing.

Yours sincerely,
Megan Buckley,
Director of
Wildlife Control

YEARLING

Turning children into readers for more than fifty

Classic and award-winning literature for every shelf.
How many have you checked out?

**Find the perfect book, play games,
and meet favorite authors at RandomHouseKids.com!**

MELONHEAD

MELONHEAD IS MY PREFERRED NAME. Preferred by me, not my mom. She likes people to call me by my real name, Adam Melon. Luckily, it's too late for that, because when my friend Lucy Rose invented Melonhead it caught on fast. Maybe because it describes my head shape.

Usually I am the one doing the inventing. All my life, which is 10 years, great ideas have been popping in and out of my melon head. Sometimes they work. This year they'd better, because our class is entering an inventing fair. My friend Sam and I are dreaming up plans. And Capitol Hill has a ton of places to find invention parts. But we have to make sure to get home on time with no excuses. That can be hard, because we have a way of forgetting. Fortunately, we know a shortcut.

MELONHEAD AND THE BIG STINK

IT WAS AN ACCIDENT—REALLY! And now that I've ruined one of Mrs. Wilkins's favorite garden plants, my parents have "loaned" me to her to do chores. This is really going to mess up my summer plans. Sam and I were going to find a way to get to New York City to see the "bunga bangkai" plant. It's twelve feet tall, weighs a hundred pounds, smells like dead mammals, and blooms once every seven years for only two days. It's the Big Stink of a Lifetime! But I have to get a few more good deeds out of the way first. Doing chores for Mrs. Wilkins is a good start, even if it wasn't in the plan to begin with!

MELONHEAD AND THE UNDERCOVER OPERATION

MELONHEAD HERE—WITH MORE RULES?! I already have the Remind-O-Rama list from my mom, which reminds me what I shouldn't do. Now my dad has created the Melon Family Guidelines for Life to remind me what I should do. And even though all these rules are so simple even a worm could follow them, I already have too much to think about.

As Junior Special Agents with the FBI, my pal Sam and I have taken a pledge—it's our duty to help apprehend a Fugitive from Justice if we spot one. And believe it or not, we've spotted one not far from where we live! The Chameleon may think she's crafty, but we can see right through her wigs, plastic noses, and putty chins. We're undercover and on the case, doing surveillance and gathering evidence. But what you see isn't always what you get!

MELONHEAD AND THE VEGALICIOUS DISASTER

FIFTH GRADE STARTED OFF WITH UNEXPECTED NEWS.
Sam, Jonique, Lucy Rose, and I have a teacher whose nickname is Bad Ms. Mad, and it already seems to fit—she gave us a homework assignment on the very first day. We felt doomed!

And now I'm doomed at home! My mom has decided I'm not eating enough vegetables, so she's using recipes that hide the vegetables under another part of the food. Sam, Pip, and I thought up a plan to get around the vegetable eating thing, but it backfired!

Finally, I would have completely forgotten—if Lucy Rose hadn't reminded me—that I have a big project for Bad Ms. Mad due tomorrow. Luckily, Lucy Rose gave me the name of a famous dead person to write about. Wait until you read what this guy is famous for—you won't believe it!

MELONHEAD AND THE WE-FIX-IT COMPANY

ANYBODY WHO IS ELEVEN NEEDS AN ALLOWANCE. My parents don't agree. Neither do Sam's. You would think they would, because due to a snafu, Sam and I have to raise some money. So we started the We-Fix-It Company and posted flyers: *You lose it, we find it. You want it, we get it. You buy it, we haul it. You grow it, we mow it. You need it, we build it.*

Requests started pouring in. Then we received the request that changed everything.